Lands of Snow and Sunset

Rachel Avery

To my father, who always said I could. I love you Dad!

Contents

Chapter One

Grayden rubbed his temples. It was getting worse. Grain was becoming scarce and inland fighting between the kingdoms on the borders had started. He pushed his dark hair from his forehead as Tumwalt continued.

"We've also noticed the nights are getting longer, which I'm sure is not news to you. The balance between sun and shadow is faltering. If we don't act now—"

"I've told you before, Tumwalt, I will not consider her proposal. It would be the end of the Snow Lands and the peace my parents strived for before their death. I will not have their legacy ruined and their kingdom fall apart." Grayden tipped back in his polished mahogany chair. "Besides," he lowered his voice, "I've been hearing odd things from the outer edges of the realm. The air is different. The past few weeks, things have been...stirring. Rumor has it there are spots on the edge of the Snow Land where magic is flowing once more. Ice Flowers have returned and the elkten are once again grazing on them."

Tumwalt exhaled audibly and raised a bushy eyebrow. He looked incredibly tailored and put together in his pressed cream tunic and neatly trimmed beard. Sometimes he still treated Grayden as the boy who had grown up playing under his father's desk in this very room, even though it had been almost five years since Grayden started overseeing the lands in his father's place.

1

"Magic? In the outer edges? There's no more power there than there is in the human realms. Surely this is just the work of the local magistrates trying to spark hope in the villages that have been hit hardest in the fading."

Grayden didn't bother to argue, and stared down at the heaps of parchment on his desk. Tumwalt was a pragmatist and no amount of gossip or hope would sway him from pushing Grayden towards a marriage alliance with the Shadow Queen, Cressida. At least Tumwalt stopped the nonsense talk of a match between Cressida's cruel cousin, Brandle, and Grayden's younger sister, Selenia. Not only was Brandle a cruel man with unknown parentage, his carnage during the Fae war was infamous. He wouldn't subject Selenia to a hateful and vicious man. Although he might have to strike a political marriage for himself one day, he hoped Selenia would marry for love. Perhaps, with the stirrings of magic on the outer edges, the land would flourish again and maybe Selenia would find her fated match. The last fated marriage known in his kingdom was his parents'. Young King Efferon had been riding on patrol in the farming lands of the river folk when something inside him sprung to life and he felt her. Grayden's mother.

At once, he knew Elowyn was his. Without even seeing her, he felt their bond and love. He raced through the village and straight into her house, still upon his horse. Grayden's grandmother had long resented Efferon for bringing the mess of the horse into her home. The young king got down on one knee and asked the pretty farmer's daughter to marry him before they even shared a meal together.

It was a story Grayden heard many times growing up, both before his parents' death and after. They'd gather around the fire in the great hall and listen to the story again and again. Grayden's mother would sketch and his father would carve little pieces of wood while their children would listen to the story they'd tell. His father would embellish his prowess and his wife's desire for him, and Grayden's mother would laugh. The Snowden siblings had grown up with tales of the great love between King Efferon and Queen Elowyn. The love that bore them not one, not two, but three children. Practically unheard of during the last two hundred years. Only the most magical of Fae were able to produce children with powers, and in recent years, few children were born, and even fewer with magical abilities. Grayden's older brother, Phillippe, was born without magic entirely. Selenia's magic was unpredictable and unstable. It was strong, but magic without control was dangerous. During the last few years, she'd stopped using it altogether after accidentally setting her own living quarters on fire. Her snowy songbird perished in the blaze and Selenia blamed herself and her magic.

In the Snowden line, Grayden's magic was the most powerful, but still it continued to fade gradually with the land. Although he was not the first born, Grayden still took on most of the responsibility for governing the Snow Lands. He had a sense of righteousness and a fairness the inhabitants of their lands trusted.

Phillippe, on the other hand, was a leader of men. And by men, mainly soldiers. He was away for long periods of time, securing borders and keeping the peace threatening to fall as the land died and the rivers and seas receded. As the eldest child, Phillippe should be the choice prospect for Queen Cressida's proposal, but his lack of magic meant any heirs he sired would be unmagical and therefore unfit to rule. This left Grayden as king all but in name. Yet he refused to usurp his brother and instead dismissed the title entirely. He kept his boyhood name, Prince Grayden of the Snow Lands, and he and Phillippe oversaw their kingdom together.

Occasionally, they differed in opinions and fought on issues: first, battling out the issue with grand debates before their advisory cabinet and then afterwards on the battlefield. Equally matched in fighting skill, they took turns gaining the upper hand. Although Grayden could theoretically use his magic to tip their melees in his favor, he never did. Such was the respect and love he had for his older brother. They managed a good balance since their father's death, but it had forced both brothers to grow up too fast.

Grayden took another deep sigh and looked at Tumwalt squarely. "For now, send more provisions to the outer edges and as many soldiers as we can afford to keep the peace," he commanded.

Tumwalt, sensing his dismissal, bowed his head slightly and left Grayden's sitting chamber.

Grayden moved to his inner bedchamber and looked out the window. Already, the sun was setting, and it was hardly past midafternoon. The stronger the Shadow Queen grew, the more his realm suffered. He feared for the time when shadow would engulf his entire land. Yet he knew a marriage alliance would only secure Queen Cressida the additional resources she desired to continue her path of war and destruction. She wouldn't be content until she ruled all the lands in the Fae world.

He caught movement out of the corner of his eye from the large floor-to-ceiling windows; he looked down at the garden and smiled as Selenia scooped up a snowball and launched it at Jurel, her private guard. Always watching her, Jurel wasn't surprised but pretended to be caught off guard at the impact against his broad chest. Selenia's red hair whipped in the wind, sending the silver snowflakes that landed on it up in a flurry, her burgundy cape swishing around her ankles as she giggled.

The castle staff adored Selenia and loved to be the object of her amusement. Her birth was unexpected and a cause for much joy. Many took it as a sign the magic in the realm was growing, even though the years had proven the theory false. Selenia's laugh was melodious, and she had a string of suitors at her disposal. None of them, in Grayden's eyes, were good enough for her pure heart. Selenia seemed to reject all suitors as well. She'd rather read in the library, shop in the village or sing and write her own songs. However, her greatest pleasure in life seemed to be annoying her older brothers. She was sweet, but a prankster. Her good nature meant that she could con the staff into playing along with her jokes, and she bested the brothers more often than they cared to admit. All the Snowden siblings had a fondness for teasing each other, but they never doubted their fierce loyalty to each other, no matter how many times Selenia managed to get live animals into their rooms or convince a hall boy to switch all their furniture, and even remove their doors from the hinges.

As Grayden watched Selenia run after Jurel, a snowball raised in her hand, he couldn't help but think about the problems at the borders. The trouble would be at their own gates soon. He needed to secure the land and somehow restore the magic before they lost it forever to the fade and shadows. He needed a miracle, but had no idea where he would find one.

Chapter Two

R enya was nothing if not an observer. Eyes slightly raised over her laptop screen, she peered intently across the street as an elderly man, dressed eccentrically in a velvet suit, closed his tattered umbrella and pushed open the door to the bookstore. Despite the pounding rain, Renya could faintly hear the bell on the door twinkle softly. The windows were fogged and Renya couldn't see anything once a customer disappeared into the warm confines of the building. Aptly named The Rainy-Day Bookstore, it was one of the oldest buildings in Seattle, and the owner was shrouded in mystery. Renya had searched business records, archives, interviewed people who worked for the city, basically pulling out every trick she knew as a journalist, but she found herself unusually stumped by this building and its mysterious owner.

She sighed as she watched the wooden door, the bookstore's name etched into it, close gently. She knew he wouldn't come back out. The ones donning old-fashioned clothes or furs or some kind of odd apparel never resurfaced. A businessman or a mother with kids in tow would go in and come out a while later with their recyclable tote bags full of reading material. But despite watching this building for the past two weeks, Renya did not see the oddities leave. She wondered if they were living in the top level of the building. Perhaps a basement? Even so, they would have to leave sometime, wouldn't they? She counted at least eight men and women in the past week who entered the store without leaving. They often wore strange hats, vintage in style and large coats in strange materials. She thought one of the men must have come directly from a renaissance fair, but she looked online and couldn't find any mention of one. Sometimes it was hard to tell if they were men or women by their dress. One individual tipped his large bowler hat to everyone passing by before he sauntered into the shop. Another woman was walking what Renya swore was some kind of iguana on a leash. She rubbed her eyes hard before the woman entered the store, not believing what she saw as its tongue darted out while the creature's stubby little legs moved in tandem.

Maybe the patrons left at night, while Renya slept underneath her thick down comforter across the street, above the warm and inviting coffee shop. She should stay up and investigate fully, but her move left her exhausted and cranky. Her only comfort was the blissful, dreamless sleep she had.

She missed the sunshine of Los Angeles and shivered as she watched a steady stream of water pour off the awning above her head. Renya missed the beaches and the palm trees, the warm ocean, and occasional celebrity sightings. She missed the quiet companionship of her Aunt Agatha and drinking tea on the large wrap-around porch. She'd have to call her tonight and check in on her. Renya had worried about leaving her aging aunt and moving up north to Seattle, but after the incident, she had no choice if she wanted to salvage her career and her life.

Space. She needed space and time to put between her and...she hated even thinking about it. Her cheeks reddened in embarrassment despite the chill in the air.

Unfortunately, working as a freelance writer was getting her nowhere and if things didn't improve and she couldn't find anyone to publish her articles, she'd either have to move home or resort to working for Tom, the owner of The Bean Coffee Shop below her apartment. He'd offered her a few shifts when he saw her surviving off of popcorn and diet soda. She'd refused, just because she didn't want to have something to fall back on. If she got too comfortable, she would stop writing and she needed the push, especially right now.

At least she could start anew in the Pacific Northwest. If Seattle wasn't far enough, there was always Alaska...

A car sped by a little too near and tossed up a large pool of water at Renya's feet, soaking her last pair of dry boots. Shivering, she decided it was time to head back upstairs. The mystery of The Rainy-Day Bookstore would have to wait. She gathered up her laptop and books, tucked her long blonde hair behind her ear, and headed for the entrance of The Bean. She pushed open the heavy oak door and was hit with the heavenly aroma of coffee. Renya breathed deep and nodded a greeting to one of the many university students who worked there. The girl smiled at Renya as she poured foam on top of a latte for a customer.

Renya scooted around the mismatched tables and plush armchairs and went behind the counter and to the backroom. She passed Tom's dark, unkempt office and headed up the poky backstairs to the tiny converted apartment. Tom lived upstairs too, along with Brianna, one of the university students who couldn't get on-campus housing after switching from a community college mid-semester. The three units were separated by locked doors, but the close quarters and shared kitchen space sometimes made for awkward conversations in the mornings. Brianna had her fair share of friends over, with some of the male ones sneaking out well past midnight. Some stayed the night and made forced conversation with Renya and Tom in the morning. If the rent checks cashed and the tenants (and their guests) left the till alone, Tom didn't seem to mind. He was pretty good natured and was a good landlord and boss to his employees.

Renya opened the door to her studio apartment and dropped her laptop bag next to the sofa. Her purse went on to the little tabletop kitchenette that held just a hot plate and an unused coffee maker. Tom was always generous with free cappuccinos, for which Renya was incredibly grateful. It rendered the tiny coffee maker useless, however.

She unlaced her boots and placed them near the small radiator, hoping to dry them before tomorrow. She grabbed a bottle of water from the mini fridge and crashed onto the worn sofa bed. It was an ugly pea green color with yellow flowers, but the last tenant left it and Renya was grateful she didn't have to spend what little savings she had on a bed set. Plus, the cramped six hundred square foot room afforded hardly any space.

She closed her eyes and let out a deep breath. So far, this move wasn't going as she had planned. She searched online for job openings, proactively sent out her portfolio unsolicited, and joined networking groups, but she couldn't even seem to land a job interview. Renya was also incredibly lonely. She had dumped Twitter, Facebook, and Instagram two weeks ago. Renya missed even the smallest social interactions with acquaintances on the web. She found herself with a lot more free time without feeds and pictures to scroll through.

Grabbing her cell phone, she pressed the button to call her aunt.

"Renya!" her aunt exclaimed. Although she was old enough to be Renya's grandmother, her eyes still sparkled and her voice was youthful. "How have you been, Sunshine?"

Renya smiled at the nickname. She instantly felt warmth radiate from her aunt's voice, filling the small room as if she was there.

"Cold and wet," she answered with a sigh.

"You could always come home..." her aunt started. Aunt Agatha had been completely against Renya's move north. When Renya broached the topic after the newspapers came out with the story between her and the senator, Aunt Agatha was firmly against her leaving. She argued day and night for a solid week. When that approach didn't change Renya's mind, she froze her out and refused to speak to her. Sadly, for Aunt Agatha, neither tactic worked, and within a month, Renya had rented out the small studio apartment and flown into Sea-Tac.

"You know I can't come home," Renya said, exasperated. "The story will follow me as long as I'm there. I'll never be able to publish anything under my real name again in LA, even if I managed to get hired anywhere."

After the scandal broke out, Renya hid low in her aunt's house, which was near Pine Mountain and an hour away from the city. Still, they found her. Journalists far and wide across the state wanted to know how a married senator was linked with a pretty twenty-four-year-old woman.

She had been foolish. He never saw her for her talent, like she believed. Her naïveté had been an embarrassment, and fleeing was her only option. She'd tried to write a rebuttal and tell her side of the story, but it didn't matter. It remained unpublished. People wanted sensationalism, not truth. 'Twenty-Four-Year-Old Homewrecker' sold more papers than 'Naïve Junior Writer Gets in Too Deep.' And if Renya was being totally honest, she fled out of sheer embarrassment, too. She was fired from her first real writing job and even her most loyal friends from college stopped returning her calls.

Aunt Agatha sighed and moved off the topic. She knew it was a sore subject for them both. "So tell me, girl, is that landlord of yours staying clear?"

A slight smile played on Renya's lips. Tom was easily sixty years old, a lifelong bachelor, and never looked at her twice. Still, Agatha was extremely protective of Renya and scrutinized all the people in her life, both men and women alike.

"Tom is like a grandpa to me, I assure you," Renya chuckled, "and I'm working on a new story. There's this bookstore across from my apartment that's kind of strange. People dressed in all sorts of weird garb show up and never leave, as far as I can tell. I can't find a record of the business owner, or even the building owner. When I asked about it at city hall, the planning commissioner acted like he had no idea what building I was even talking about," Renya finished.

There was silence on the line. Three, four, five seconds came and went.

"Hello? Auntie? Are you still there?"

Aunt Agatha's voice came in a rush. "Sunshine, you stay far away from anything like that. Don't stick your nose in business that's not yours. Look where it got you in LA. If you'd kept your head down, you wouldn't be where you are. A thousand miles away from me and no one to protect you. Find a nice job at a newspaper and write obituaries or advice columns. Or better yet, come home and get married and have some babies. Have a nice family and leave the worries to your husband."

Aunt Agatha's words both stung and shocked her. She had never once implied Renya was to blame for the scandal. Even when a reporter crossed into Aunt Agatha's yard and smashed through her prized herb garden, she was nothing but sympathetic towards Renya's plight and indignant at the treatment of her niece. She knew Renya did nothing wrong, other than believe a powerful man was going to help her in her career for nothing in return.

Her aunt's words were also extremely hypocritical. Never, in the twenty-four years she'd lived with Aunt Agatha, had a man ever been in their house. Self reliance was a virtue for her aunt, and even in her old age, she refused to let anyone else shovel her walkway or fix a broken appliance. And someone to protect her? This was coming from the woman who had put Renya into Girl Scouts and martial arts and taken her into the forest and showed her how to live off the land? Renya choked back a surprised gasp.

"I've got to go. It's late and I have some stories to send out." She didn't want her aunt to hear her cry. Strength was always a virtue she highly valued in Renya. But right now Renya was tired, cold and defeated.

"Sunshine, I'm sorry but—"

"It's okay. I'll call next week, okay?"

Renya ended the call even as her aunt tried to apologize and threw the phone on the floor before the tears ran down her cheeks. She pulled her knees against her chest and hugged herself and let the tears fall.

The rain dripped outside her apartment window, and across the street, the man in the velvet suit never appeared again.

Chapter Three

G rayden rushed out of the great hall and into the courtyard as soon as he saw the ashy-colored hawk circling from the window. By the time he arrived in the courtyard, the magnificent bird was already perched on a low wall and a stableboy was removing the parchment secured to her ankle. As soon as she was free from her charge, the hawk rose towards the snowy mountains behind them, disappearing. The boy handed the crumpled letter to Grayden. He quickly flipped it over and saw it bore Phillippe's seal: a snowy white owl. This was not what Grayden was expecting; he was hoping for some kind of communication from his double-agent in the Shadow Queen's court.

Grayden broke the seal and his eyes skimmed the letter as fast as he could. Danger. Reinforcements needed. Attack. Soldiers hurt. Send help. Now.

Before anyone could ask what was going on, Grayden's deep voice was shouting orders.

"Saddle my horse! At once! And our best healer! All soldiers who are able need to prepare to ride south within the hour!"

The people in the courtyard jumped to attention, carrying out tasks as Grayden continued his authoritative commands. "Find Princess Selenia and Captain Jurel immediately and have them brought to me! And find Tumwalt!"

Grayden didn't even allow himself a second to make sure his orders were being followed. He hurried back into the lodge and up the grand staircase, taking the stairs two at a time, storming towards his bedchamber. Rounding the corner, he ran right into Tumwalt, who was carrying a large stack of rolled parchment.

"My lord, what is happening?" Tumwalt asked in a rush.

"Phillippe and his troops were ambushed along the southern border. It appears as though the Shadow Queen has sent her army to thin our resources. Or perhaps this is the start of a battle for territory. Honestly, I'm not sure what she's after..." he trailed off, already frowning at the lack of intelligence they received about her motives.

"Have we not heard anything from Sion?" Tumwalt asked, following Grayden into his chambers.

"No, absolutely nothing since he mentioned he was going to seduce her. He also wrote in his last letter he was concerned Queen Cressida was starting to suspect his double role. Maybe he's being followed and couldn't get a message out."

Grayden began shucking his clothes and changing into warm furs. He opened a cabinet and pulled out a long sword with a jeweled hilt.

"This is not good, Tumwalt," he continued. "With no inside information, I fear we may be heading into a trap." He pinched the bridge of his nose. Fates, why did it have to be now? The magic he had performed last week to refreeze a quickly melting glacier threatening the northernmost village had left him both depleted and exhausted. It would be at least a fortnight before he regained any usable power. He could barely summon a small flurry and even trying left him hardly able to stand.

He cursed inwardly as he swung the long fur over his shoulders.

"How do you wish to proceed?" Tumwalt asked.

Grayden pulled on his tall riding boots, slipping a small diamond tipped dagger into his right boot and slinging his sword and sheath over his shoulder. At six feet tall, he was a daunting creature, but prepared for battle, he looked downright frightening. "I need you to rule in my name until I can sort this out and figure out what's going on. Go see if Almory had any visions or stirrings that might explain her sudden attack. And for Fate's sake, is he any closer to finding the meaning of that prophecy? Gods, we need a miracle."

Tumwalt lowered his eyes. He knew Almory's visions were becoming less accurate and disappearing altogether. As for the prophecy, Almory had yet to decipher the golden, scrolling text.

"The language on the scroll still moves too fast for him to even translate it into any real meaning. He thinks it might be early elvenish, but even then, he can only translate a letter here and there before the text disappears altogether. He says it's almost as if the scroll is placed under a confusion spell, besides being under a guardian ritual."

Grayden cursed aloud this time as he hurried out of his chambers. What good was finding the blasted scroll if they had no way of revealing the truth it held? Legends told it alone held the key to restoring the balance between all the realms. With the Shadow Queen's power mounting, time was running out.

Jurel appeared in the hall. "My lord, you summoned me? I heard there is going to be a battle. Shall I accompany you as your private guard?"

"No, Jurel. I need you here, looking out for what is most dear to me."

"I'm guessing you don't mean Tumwalt?" Jurel raised his eyebrows as Grayden gave him a look. "Don't worry, no harm will come to the princess while I breathe."

"I trust her life with you, Jurel. And her virtue. Don't forget it."

Jurel scowled. He'd known both Grayden and Selenia since they were all children together and he would allow nothing untoward to happen. "You know I would never touch her."

"It's not necessarily you I worry about." The last year or so Grayden had noticed a closeness between the pair. Jurel was a distant man, sometimes harsh and impenetrable. It was the main reason Grayden had assigned him to watch over Selenia. But his frosty exterior had melted in her presence. He doubted Jurel encouraged the flirtatious behavior, but he knew Selenia was persuasive and could be downright devious when she wanted something bad enough. Perhaps it was time to reassign him...but right now he needed her kept safe until he returned, and there was no one better for the job than Jurel. He didn't doubt his loyalty. The pair continued down the stairs in silence, each absorbed in their own thoughts.

Selenia met them at the bottom of the staircase as Grayden prepared to take his leave.

"What's going on?" she asked, a worried look on her face.

"Selenia, Phillippe is in danger. I'm riding out to help. I'll send word as soon as I can."

With a quick kiss on the top of her head, he grumbled to her to behave herself, and then prayed to the gods he would live to see her again.

Chapter Four

Despite Aunt Agatha's warning and condescension, Renya woke up with renewed determination to find out what was going on in the bookstore. It was like an itch in her mind and no matter how many times she tried to scratch it, she couldn't rid herself of the feeling it was a mystery she had to solve. She got off of the sofa bed she had folded down and went over to the tiny closet that held her clothes. Renya desperately needed to go shopping. As a native Californian, she was severely underdressed for the dreary and constant rain of the Pacific Northwest. She rummaged through pairs of shorts and tank tops and managed to find a dress. Sighing, she located her last pair of leggings and put them on under the dress. Luckily, her boots were dry after spending the night near the radiator, and Renya laced them up. She pulled her hair up and threw on a little make-up, but did not bother to hide the patch of freckles under her eyes. Renya had a similar patch on the back of her neck, and as a child, Aunt Agatha told her it was where the stork bit her. She usually kept her hair down, but she was tired of the ends being wet all the time, so she secured it back away from her face. She grabbed her laptop bag and a few granola bars and went downstairs to the bustle of the early morning rush at The Bean.

The rich aroma of coffee hit her nose the second she opened her door. That was one plus of living above a coffee shop; it always smelled inviting and comforting. She hurried down the stairs and through the small kitchen into the main room. The Bean was packed with students from the university, all seeking a jolt of caffeine before their classes started and their professors bored them to death with statistics and history, literature and calculus.

Brianna was working the morning shift and as soon as Renya came to the counter, she pushed a steaming hot latte into her hands. Renya smiled appreciatively as she clutched the toasty cup in her chilly hands.

"What are you up to today, Renya?" Brianna asked, as she wiped up a spill on the counter with a threadbare rag. She wore a tiny blue apron over her university sweatshirt. Her tidy brown hair was French braided and her black glasses slipped down her nose slightly as the steam from the cappuccino machine hit her face.

"The usual. I'm going to sit outside and try to write and send off a few more spec pieces. Maybe go to the bookstore across the street." She tried to sound nonchalant as she blew on the top of her drink to cool it. "How about you?"

"Same old, same old," Brianna replied with a lazy smile. "Make coffee, go to class, study, sleep, repeat."

"I'm pretty sure there are a few boys in the mix too," Renya teased.

Brianna chuckled knowingly. "Yeah, some of that too..." She turned back to the counter to take an order from a customer who was huffing impatiently. Brianna waved a quick, apologetic goodbye to Renya.

Renya looked at the pouring rain pounding against The Bean's front windows and cringed inwardly.

Surveying the room, she saw an open armchair next to the window with a good view of the bookstore. She knew Tom didn't like it when she took up customer space, but she just needed a few minutes in the warmth to finish her drink before heading across the street. Plus, it was almost 9:00 a.m. and the bulk of the college students would soon head out to class, work-study jobs, or their dorm room to study. Renya missed those days. She did well in school and almost everything academic came easily to her. She kept herself busy, writing for the university's newspaper and working part time in the Dean's office. Now, with no job, she felt idle and unsure of herself. Losing her job had been a tremendous blow to her ego, and it shook how she identified herself. She was a good girl who never got in trouble. Now she had been fired, unfriended, and was the subject of salacious gossip. It wasn't exactly what she had pictured for her life.

Renya leaned back into the plush velvet chair and riffled through her laptop bag. She pulled out one of the strawberry granola bars and chewed thoughtfully, her mind already focusing on the bookstore across the street. Another ten minutes and it would be open. Renya wanted to wait to look around the store until there were a few customers inside. Hopefully, she'd be able to investigate without being bothered by a sales clerk.

Finishing her coffee, she tightened her thin pink windbreaker around her and braced herself for the onslaught of rain. She opened the door and instantly regretted leaving the warmth and comfort of the velvet chair. Still, strengthened by resolve, she walked purposefully across the street, careful to avoid the oil-slick puddles.

As she pushed open the door to The Rainy-Day

Bookstore and heard the familiar twinkling bell at the door, her writer's instincts took over and she caught herself slowly taking in everything and etching every detail in her mind.

So far, a normal bookstore. A slight musty smell, not unusual for an old building in a soggy climate. The register was right up front, but rather than a sales counter, it stood on an antique desk. An aging library cart stood next to it, filled with used books. A collection of journals and stationary were set up near a large self-help section. Renya wondered if there were any self-help books about what to do when your world came crashing down around you and you felt like an epic failure. If not, maybe she should write one.

The books in the window were mostly popular best sellers: a memoir by a famous TV star detailing her spiral into drug addiction, a classic novel recently adapted into a movie, thus creating a market for the nearly forgotten book, and a set of encyclopedias. Renya suppressed a snort when she saw the encyclopedias. Whoever ordered for this store might be slightly out of touch with the modern world if they thought anyone had a use for a set of Britannica encyclopedias.

The store itself was actually quite charming and welcoming. Wood paneling lined the walls, and there were seating areas strategically placed for patrons to leaf through a book or decide what they wanted to purchase. A few steps led up to a raised level and Renya realized right away there really wasn't a second story. Instead, the shop appeared to have three levels separated by just a handful of steps as it sprawled towards the back. It surprised Renya how large it was; the store appeared smaller from the street and much more dilapidated on the outside.

She climbed the narrow steps to the second level and noticed the books on this level were all used books. She sighed happily, taking in the smell of well-loved books. There was nothing better than that smell. As a writer, Renya also devoured books. The only reason she hadn't entered the store when she first arrived in Seattle was because of her financial situation; the credit card in her wallet was for emergencies only. No matter how hard she tried, she just couldn't convince herself leaving all of her books behind warranted a shopping spree, so she tried to ignore the temptation and had read free classics on her phone at night.

Renya slowly traced the spine of an aged Jane Austen book and then scolded herself. She'd already forgotten why she was there. She wanted to find out what was happening here and if there was a story worth telling. Renya walked past the stacks of historical fiction books and headed up to the third level.

Here, temptation struck her again, and she swore her hands trembled as she saw what lay before her. These weren't just old or used books. These were treasures.

Stored in locked display cases stood the largest collection of rare books Renya had seen. She approached the first shelf, dropped her bag, and peered inside. An ancient copy of Dante's Inferno stared back at her. Oh, how she longed to open it and see the illustrations! And next to it, equally impressive to her, at least, was an early edition of Common Sense. Her heart leapt as she took in the plethora of rare publications.

Instantly, she knew how wrong she'd been. A peace came over her as she stalked the glass cases, glancing at the titles in wonderment. Nothing sinister could happen here. In fact, how could she bring herself to leave? She couldn't blame anyone for spending hours here. She imagined herself passing the day away, curled in one of the many chairs, tucked away between the stacks. How very tempting the picture was!

"I see you've found my pride and joy," a warm voice came from behind her.

Renya squeaked and twisted around. An older man, impeccably dressed in a charcoal suit, stood leaning against a bookshelf.

She regained her composure. "You have an amazing collection. How did you come by all these rare books? I've never seen so many first editions in one place before."

His blue eyes danced as he smiled. "When you've been around as long as I have, dear, you learn how to acquire the things you long for the most. Things you thought were long gone. Things you gave up on and never thought you'd live to see."

Renya looked at him, puzzled by his lofty statement. His eyes twinkled, and he winked at her. "I have a private buyer who goes to auctions around the world for me," he explained, laughing slightly at her gullibility.

Renya stood dumbfounded as he grabbed a set of keys from inside his suit jacket and moved towards the glass case Renya had been looking in just moments before. He unlocked it, reached inside, and pulled out a book from the back. He outstretched his arms, and Renya glimpsed his sparkling golden cufflinks before she took the book into her trembling palms.

One of the first copies of The Tales of Peter Rabbit rested in her hands. Renya gasped in surprise and nearly dropped the precious book. The owner looked at her reaction with pride.

"It's a favorite," he explained. "A good friend related to Beatrix Potter gave this copy to me. They gave these to Potter to distribute to friends and family. One of my prized possessions. Go on, take a look. I'll be at the front if you have any questions." He locked the display case and added, "we also have quite the collection in the basement as well. Bargain books for any budget."

Renya numbly turned a page and backed into the chair behind her. She wiped her hands on her dress as if they were covered in grime. She wished she had a pair of cloth gloves to wear when turning the delicate pages. The man smiled and turned on his heels and headed back down the stairs to the front of the store.

The Tales of Peter Rabbit was her favorite book growing up. Aunt Agatha would read it to her every night before bed. How amazing to find such a rare copy!

One of her literature professors had a fondness for rare books and introduced Renya to the beauty of them. Oh, how she wished she could show her! Smiling, she reached for her cell phone and turned the pages, snapping pictures to send to Dr. Irving when she got back to her apartment. She would be so pleased. Renya knew she would pepper her with all kinds of questions. It would be nice to have someone to talk to who wouldn't bring up the scandal with the senator.

A half hour passed before Renya even noticed. She sighed, knowing she needed to get busy writing if she wanted to make rent next month.

She went to the front of the store, cradling Peter Rabbit in her arms as if the book was a real rabbit, and searched around for the man so she could return the precious book. She looked by the register and in between the shelves. However, he wasn't anywhere to be seen. She didn't even see any other customers.

Frowning, Renya turned around and called out. "Hello? Is anyone here?" When she received no response, she took the book and placed it on the chair behind the desk holding the register. She hated to leave it out and quickly changed her mind, dropping it into her laptop bag.

Renya noticed how quiet the store had become. When she had entered, there were at least four or five other customers here, but now she was completely alone. A chill ran through her spine, and a sense of foreboding came over her.

When she was seven years old, she was in a car crash with her aunt and remembered seeing the car come hurtling towards their car and she knew she couldn't prevent the impact. Now Renya braced herself for some unknown derailment, all of her senses heightened. She tried her best to suppress the sudden urge of paranoia. It was just a bookstore. And this was just like any other day.

The owner had mentioned a basement; perhaps he was there. She'd rather return the book directly to him. And just maybe, if she scrimped this month, she could afford a couple of bargain books. She was getting her coffee for free, after all.

She weaved around a few more bookshelves and saw a sign pointing the way to the basement. There was a lock and a deadbolt on the door, and a chain at the top. Weird, she thought, especially since this is where the bargain books were supposed to be. She opened the unlocked door and headed down the worn, wooden stairs. They creaked and worried with each careful step.

At the landing, she saw a long corridor with old-fashioned wallpaper lining the walls. Pink and yellow flowers on top of a candy striped pattern stuck out as odd to her. It looked almost Victorian. Not what she would expect in the basement of a bookstore. Renya was instantly confused. Where were the bargain books? She reached for the first door in the long hall, but she found it locked. Frowning, she took a step forward and her heart lurched.

Perspiration dripped down her forehead and the back of her neck burned and tingled. The hallway suddenly blazed with brightness and at the end of the passageway, one door stood out. It almost seemed to glow, and Renya was inexplicably drawn to it. She ignored the other doors, some adorned with carvings of flowers, shells, animals, and various other symbols. She hardly noticed them. Without thinking, she crept towards the golden door. Every step seemed important, as if this was a path she was deliberately meant to walk. This was the moment her whole life had been pointing to. With every step, she felt a stronger and stronger pull, as if gravity was no longer pulling her towards the earth but spiraling her towards this door and whatever truth lay beyond it.

Approaching the door, she shakily pressed both hands against the smooth wood and swore she felt the door vibrate when her palms made contact. Her heart matched the beat of the pulsation and for the briefest of moments, she didn't know where she began and the door ended, so entwined was their fate.

As if possessed, she turned her head and placed her cheek flush against the shining door. A small, worn carving caught her eye. She traced it with her finger lightly, trying to discern what it was. A star? The sun? A snowflake? She couldn't tell, but she continued to run her fingers gently over it, caressing it like a lover.

Chest pounding, her heart leaped again and all at once, she knew she desperately needed what was on the other side of this door. She didn't know it, but something had been missing from her, and whatever it was, it was on the other side of this door. A part of her ached, and a longing hit her so hard it was almost painful. But there was clarity too, and she knew everything would make sense if she could just get beyond this door. Renya's breath caught in her chest, and her hands shook but were determined as she slowly turned the doorknob. It felt warm and sure and right under her palm. Words like destiny, fate, hope and perfection flashed across her mind. She smiled widely, feeling so much happier than she had ever been in her life as she pushed it open.

There was nothing but bright light and utter silence, and then a blast of icy wind hit her face and she stumbled forward, falling into whatever was behind the door frame.

And like all of those strangely dressed people who came to The Rainy-Day Bookstore before her, Renya was gone.

Chapter Five

R enya's entire body burned. Once, when she was a child, she bumped her leg against Aunt Agatha's wooden stove. The spot turned bright red and blistered. That was the closest sensation she could use to describe the pain she felt now. But this was a million times worse. It was like that pain was everywhere, even deep inside her body. The agony forced her into a ball with her eyes tightly shut. Her parched mouth felt brittle and her skin felt too tight for her body. The only sensation besides pain she could feel was the heat radiating off of her skin. She felt dizzy and disoriented. She kept her eyes closed and waited for the sensation of the world spinning to pass. Slowly, Renya opened her eyes.

There was whiteness everywhere. She rubbed her eyes, only to find her fingers trembling with cold. Once her body had stopped burning, the chill reached out with its icy fingers and cold overtook her. She looked around but there was nothing but tall, ancient trees and thick blankets of snow.

What had happened to her? Where was she? She couldn't even remember what had transpired. She remembered leaving The Bean, and then...

The bookstore. A man with sparkling blue eyes. A door...and a need to get to whatever was behind it? Was that what it was? She knew there was a reason she abandoned common sense and went through a mysterious door in a basement.

Her whole body shook, but not just from the temperature. How did she get here? Why was she here? This couldn't be happening. Renya lived in the real world. She didn't believe in fate or miracles, ghosts or superstitions. When thinking of the mystery of the bookstore, she assumed the reason for people disappearing from the store had something to do with fake passports or illegal cage fighting in the basement. But this? This wasn't her life.

She sat up as snowflakes swirled around her. The ground she was sitting on was wet, as if her body heat alone had melted it. She heard twigs snap and jerked her head around. Twenty feet in front of her was a snowy white deer. No, wait. Deer weren't white. What was this creature?

The animal stared back at Renya and then carefully tilted its head down to chew on some icy shoots near a fallen log. Renya breathed deeply, momentarily calmed by the presence of the creature. Its eyes were a stark gray and upon closer examination, she noticed the dappled white fur had spots of gray shaped into stars. The legs were slightly thicker than a deer and it had rounded ears, twitching slightly with its movements. Renya took another deep breath and started towards the creature, slowly.

It watched Renya carefully, slowly chewing the ice white shoots. The animal's sides moved in and out rhythmically, its breath steady and even.

"Hi pretty girl," Renya cooed. "Can you tell me where I am?"

The animal stared back at her, almost as if she expected Renya to do something. Anything. Then, as quickly as she appeared, the strange animal pranced off, its silver hooves leaving star-like shaped prints in the snow.

Renya shivered again. What was this place? Her mind thought back to her last conversation with Aunt Agatha. Was this what she was warning about? She knew her aunt could be a tad eccentric, but magic doors to other worlds? This was the stuff of fiction and fairy tales.

However, without a reasonable explanation, Renya had accepted she was no longer in her world. The strange animal, the way the snow hung in the air without ever seeming to fall...and then there was *the fall*. She fell, didn't she? There was a blast of wind, pain, and then... this. Was it a dream? The cold and pain had felt too real to be an illusion.

Renya looked behind her, and a golden archway shone bright before fading away. The door, or whatever it had been, was gone.

Okay, Renya told herself, let's say that this is true, and you are in some kind of other world or reality. What do we do? Her mind instantly sprang to the years spent in the forest with Aunt Agatha. Shelter. Water. Food. Heat. It was almost as if her aunt had been preparing her for something like this...had she been?

First things first. She needed shelter. Her clothes were severely lacking in this climate and her teeth were chattering. The perspiration that gathered on her forehead was already freezing. Yet she felt a strange warmth coming from the back of her neck. Odd. She brushed her fingers against it, and sure enough, there was heat there, almost as if it was infected. She shook the thought away and looked around the clearing. There were more pressing matters to deal with than her neck feeling warm.

Which way should she go? She guessed one way was as good as any other, but at the last second, she followed the footprints of the silvered deer. Before she started to trudge ahead, she caught sight of her laptop bag, partially hidden under the snow. Oh, how she wished it contained something useful! How she longed for matches or a lighter. If she got herself back home, she'd never travel without matches in her bag. She looked at the lone granola bar as her stomach rumbled. When did she last eat? Renya opened it, munching on it while she attempted to forge a path through the snow.

One step after another. Snow and more snow. The snowflakes whipped around her body and sometimes they were so thick it was difficult to see her way. She tried to continue along the small trail the mysterious white deer had left, but it was almost gone, snow flattening out the dainty stars. Renya's feet were numb with the cold, and her fingers were pink and stinging. Every few steps, she'd bend her fingers, trying to keep blood circulating through them.

She tried to take her mind off the cold by observing her surroundings. That's what she did when things got hard. Renya would write stories in her head, grand epic tales of mystery and adventure. She thought of what it must be like to be one of the first explorers in the poles, stepping foot on the majestic ice for the first time. Documenting everything she saw helped keep her going.

Renya heard a bird cry, but couldn't see where the sound was coming from. The trees seemed to thin out and their massive height diminished as she approached a small hill. Up one side, down the other. Renya pushed through the thick snow, her boots sinking in, and she had to wrestle them free with each step. Snow seeped inside her boots as she struggled through the larger drifts. The snow seemed to get deeper the further she went. Tears stung in her eyes before freezing in place. Did she choose wrong? Should she have gone the opposite way?

Her breathing became ragged, and each breath stung as it settled in her chest. An hour passed, maybe two. She had no way to measure the time. She kept flicking at her Apple Watch, but there was nothing on the screen. Her bag was starting to feel immensely heavy as her feet dragged in the snow, and it was getting dark and hard to see. Renya sighed, opened up the leather bag, and left her laptop on the embankment. She needed to find a shelter, and anything not helping her quest was hurting her and slowing her down. Renya thought of the copy of The Tales of Peter Rabbit in her bag. She felt like bursting into tears as she made sure she protected the book from the elements the best she could. She zipped it into an inside pocket of the laptop bag before she left it in the snow as well.

More time passed and complete darkness set in. Her eyes felt heavy, and it was so quiet. She couldn't feel her feet at all and her fingers were stiff. At some point, she must have stopped bending them. Her mind wasn't working the way it should, and she felt disoriented and confused. The cold surrounded her, and she sat down against another fallen log. She curled inward, hugging her knees and trying to blow warm air on her hands. She gave herself a little pep talk. You will not give up, she scolded. You ran away from your problems once, and you will not give up now!

Renya rose to her trembling feet and shoved herself forward. She would survive. She was a survivor.

Just a few more steps and then another hill. Perhaps on the other side of the hill there would be shelter...another painful step, and then Renya collapsed against the cool, unforgiving silver snow.

Chapter Six

T hey'd been riding hard for an entire day. Grayden looked back over his shoulder at his men and grimaced. They were in awful shape. Many sagged in the saddle, others were wide-eyed, staring off into space. The horses were dragging their heads and slowing in protest. In his quest to get to his brother, he'd neglected both his men and their beasts. He lifted a hand and Charly, his second in command, came up beside him.

"Find a place to make camp. This lot is no good to me if they are so tired they can barely stay in the saddle," he said, motioning to the thirty riders behind him. "We'll rest for a few hours and then start again at first light."

Charly nodded and began shouting orders to the rest of the men. They unloaded tents and sleeping rolls off their horses' backs and fires popped up all over the site. Grayden moved away from his men and walked off a perimeter around the makeshift camp, counting off paces and deciding how many men should guard while the others slept. He calculated how long the shifts should be with how many men. He would take every shift, of course, so more men could sleep. Phillippe was his brother and Grayden was the type of person to sacrifice himself for others. His father had been the same way.

Grayden grabbed a torch from one of the men and crept deeper into the forest, getting a sense of the terrain and any potential weaknesses that could put them in danger of an ambush. The forest was thinner here, which meant they would have a clear line of sight for any attempted attack.

He caught sight of a sliver of silver through the trees and raised his torch. His breath caught. An elkten? They were nearing the outskirts where they had been rumored to be seen. He looked down in the snow and saw the telltale star hoofprints and grinned to himself. It was true. Grayden moved forward, eager to catch a better glimpse of the animal, his tall black boots crunching the snow beneath.

He walked a few more paces, his torch lighting the way and his eyes dead ahead, looking for the animal. He was so determined to find one and prove Tumwalt wrong that he practically tripped over a log. Wait, not a log...

He lowered his torch. A pretty little girl lay collapsed in the snow at his feet. Her golden yellow hair cascaded around her in a puddle, and snow clung to her lashes. Her skin was pale with cold and Grayden could barely make out her facial features under the snow that had settled on her, but he thought he saw a few soft freckles framing her cheeks. She was not dressed for the weather, wearing some kind of pink outerwear over a long tunic with skin-tight trousers and her inadequate clothes were soaked through.

"Charly!" Grayden called. "Quick, help me!"

He stuck the base of the torch into the snow, bending down and lifting the frozen girl to his chest. "It's okay," he murmured to her. "You're safe now." The girl tried to open her eyes, but her frozen lashes prevented her. She tried to speak, but her lips had fallen victim to the same fate as her eyes. Her face was practically blue, and she appeared to be hovering near death.

"Hush, little one. Save your strength. You're in good hands," he said as she thrashed a bit in his arms. Her strength gave out quickly, and she went still as he carried her through the woods, still calling for Charly.

Charly finally appeared, shock screwing up his usually calm features. "My lord, what…" he trailed off.

"I found her a little way out. She looks to be almost frozen solid. And dressed improperly for our land. This area is uninhabited. How she got out here is a mystery—"

Another kind of shock rippled through him. Gods, was there a portal out here? Fates! If the rumors were true and there was magic again along the borders, it was possible for a portal to open. He moved the girl closer to the light from Charly's torch and looked at her more closely. Wait, this was not a child. A woman. And not Fae, he thought, as he examined her rounded ears. What realm did she come from? Did she mean to travel here? He resisted the strange urge to pull her even closer to him.

Charly looked at the woman closely. "My lord, she's…not of this world. What does it mean?"

Grayden looked at him squarely in the eyes. "It means perhaps the Fates haven't forsaken us after all."

Chapter Seven

R enya woke up slowly and tried to pull her quilt closer to her chin. She was so cold and her fingers felt stiff and heavy. She smelled smoke in the air and was glad Aunt Agatha started a fire. Winter came upon them fast in the mountains and—

She opened one of her eyes partially. The room was dark. She moved her fingers down the covering, only to feel soft fur rather than her linen quilt. As she tried to move her fingers, it all came back to her. The cold. The snow...and...what had happened to her? She vaguely remembered a man, carrying her in his arms. Where was she?

"I thought you would sleep away the nightfall." A deep voice came from the darkest corner of the room.

Startled, Renya tried to yell out, to demand to know who this man was and where he had taken her, but nothing came out. Her throat burned, and it hurt to move her lips. She tried unsuccessfully to raise herself to a sitting position. At once, there was a flutter of movement and the shadow crossed over to where she lay. The smell of pine and warm spice overwhelmed her as she tried to open her other eye. The rich voice came again and calloused, yet gentle hands pushed her back into the warm furs.

"You need to rest," the stranger commanded. From the tone and timber of his voice, Renya had the feeling this man was used to being obeyed. "You are in my camp and in my tent. I found you while walking off the perimeter of the camp and since you were in no condition to say you needed assistance, I took it upon myself to bring you back here."

Her head swam as she tried to make sense of his words. The last thing she remembered was sheer determination. She would not give up, but apparently her body had other ideas. Her arms and legs felt tingly as sensation slowly started to return. She wiggled her toes, only to realize her boots and socks had been removed. Had this man removed them? Thankfully, she was still wearing her other clothes.

The man grasped her shoulders gingerly and helped to prop her up so she could sit. She instantly felt less vulnerable now that she was upright. He held a cup of something hot and steaming to her lips.

"Drink," he commanded. "It will help warm you."

Between the darkness in the tent and her scratchy eyes, she couldn't see exactly what the cup contained. But a warm citrus scent wafted up, and she struggled to lift her head to drink. Those large and calloused hands reached behind her neck to help her lift her head. Before she could take a sip, the stranger's hands made contact with the back of her neck and heat radiated throughout her entire body before she blacked out.

Chapter Eight

"**S**o you've a woman in yer tent, and you're out with us?" one of the men teased. "Don't know what to do with her, eh?"

"Maybe he's already done his bit!" another retorted. "Did she even know you did it to her, prince?" The entire camp roared with laughter. It was obvious to Grayden that the period of rest and the fireale had perked up his men, and word about the girl had spread fast throughout their ranks.

Grayden ignored their boisterous insults as he crossed through the camp and sought out Dimitri, their healer. He found Dimitri next to one of the horses, treating a small laceration on the large animal's flank.

"I need you to come with me," Grayden said, his voice full of urgency.

Wordlessly, Dimitri patted the jet black horse on the rump and followed Grayden back to his tent. The jeers from the men continued, the conversation getting louder and more lewd by the second. The sight of the healer returning to Grayden's tent with him only made the sexual innuendo worse. Grayden made a mental note to cut back the amount of fireale he rationed out to his men.

Grayden entered his tent with Dimitri at his heels and gestured towards the unconscious woman. She had fallen back onto Grayden's furs, her head resting softly on his balled up cloak he placed under her. Dimitri moved aside his black robes, the sign of a healer, and kneeled and pressed his palm to the girl's forehead.

"I heard rumors among the men that you found a girl in the forest. What happened?"

Grayden lowered his voice, not wishing to be overheard by the bantering men outside. "I tried to help her drink some crimling tea and the second I touched her, she spasmed and collapsed. And when I touched her neck, my hand...it burned."

Dimitri didn't even bother trying to hide his surprise. "Burned? How so?"

"I don't know if burned is exactly the right word," Grayden struggled. "It was more like a strike of lightning and then a warmth coursed through my hand and spread to my chest."

Dimitri just looked puzzled at Grayden's description. "Well, let me examine her. You can wait outside." He made a movement toward the bed of furs that held the unconscious woman.

Grayden quickly put his body between the woman and the healer. Suddenly, he felt a rush of protectiveness towards this stranger. It made no sense. He didn't even know her name. She wasn't of his world or even Fae, yet he didn't want the healer to touch her. Which was... insane. Dimitri had been the one to deliver Selenia and had seen them through all of their childhood illnesses. He was trustworthy, loyal and the best healer they had.

Dimitri raised an eyebrow and gave Grayden a critical stare. He didn't question Grayden, but took a step back as Grayden sunk down on the furs and lifted the girl onto his lap so they could look at her neck together.

Grayden rested her chest against his, cradling her head and sliding her gossamer hair away from her neck so Dimitri could examine the spot from which the heat radiated.

"Quite remarkable…" Dimitri muttered to himself, tracing a spot on the girl's neck.

Grayden swallowed the growl threatening to erupt from his lips as Dimitri touched her. "What's remarkable?" Grayden spat out a little too harshly.

Dimitri ignored his tone. "She's been marked by Fae magic. Here, on the back of her neck, you see?" Grayden shifted the woman so he could look down at her neck. The shape of a sun shone golden on her warm skin. Gods, marked by magic? First, a portal opening and then a creature comes through it, having been marked by their magic?

Grayden cleared his throat, somewhat hesitantly. He felt almost foolish, like he was imagining this connection he felt to her. "Did the mark feel…warm to your touch?"

Dimitri frowned and put his palm fully on the mark. "No," he answered simply, waiting for Grayden to elaborate. When he didn't, Dimitri glanced back down at the mysterious girl.

Grayden resisted the urge to touch her neck again to see if he could replicate the heat he had experienced. If the slight touch he gave her was enough to render her unconscious, he didn't want to take any chances of harming her further. He laid her back down on the furs and arranged her soft hair and tucked the furs around her as if she was a precious infant. If Dimitri was puzzled by his gentleness and care of the girl, he didn't remark.

"How soon until she gains consciousness?" Grayden asked, gnawing on his bottom lip. Every second he lingered here at camp meant more time his brother was outnumbered, taken hostage, or possibly dead. On the other hand, a girl marked by magic needed to be protected and taken back to his castle to Almory.

"It's hard to say, my lord. Are you thinking of bringing her with us?"

Grayden stared past Dimitri to the woman with the golden hair laying upon his furs. She stirred and mumbled a bit, and he was glad that she seemed to be coming around. He watched her lips part, her breathing deep and felt something...unknown stir within him. It wasn't lust, but something deeper.

"Well, I won't leave her here, that's for damn certain."

Chapter Nine

T his time, when she awoke, Renya knew exactly where she was. No longer dark, light seeped into the tent and her eyes adjusted to the brightness. She blinked a few times, testing her vision and breathing a sigh of relief when it was clear. She sat up and looked around. It was the same room as last night, although now she recognized it as a large tent with a pole in the middle and a small fire burning in the center. That explained the smoke she smelled earlier. A flap at the roof of the tent let the smoke escape while the fire crackled and hissed. A dark navy traveling trunk lay in the corner, along with what looked like a sword with jewels dazzling the hilt. The smell of fresh wood and pine hit her nose again, and she turned to her left to find the same man from last night sitting on a small log next to her. Piercing emerald eyes met hers, and a rush of warmth slid down her body as those knowing eyes appraised her. She cleared her throat, but the stranger spoke first.

"How are you fairing?" he asked, his voice deep and resonating. Renya tested her own voice.

"I'm..." she trailed off. How was she? So far she'd fallen through some kind of door into another world, nearly frozen to death, and had woken up in a strange man's tent. But she was alive. That was something, right?

The man's penetrating gaze locked eyes with hers yet again. He cleared his throat and leaned forward with his elbows on his knees. The stranger was a broad man, with wide shoulders and thick muscles. He was wearing a simple gray tunic with a silver emblem on the collar. Renya tried to make it out...a fox, perhaps? Or a deer? She glanced at his face. He had a strong jaw, with just a hint of brown scruff and a mop of wild, unruly hair falling just over his eyes and curled around his face. Under any other circumstance, Renya was sure she would have found him attractive. However, given her recent mistrust of men, his favorable looks did him no favors in her eyes.

He didn't take his piercing eyes off of her as he began speaking. "I'm the lord of these lands, and my men and I are on course to reach our southern borders. We are on our way to a battle where I expect much bloodshed and carnage. We stopped to rest when I found you, collapsed in the snow. I don't mean to rush you, and I know you are most likely disoriented, but do you think you can ride?"

What...ride? Renya was having trouble comprehending his words. She shook her head as if to clear her muddled thoughts. The man took it to mean that no, she wasn't able to ride.

"If you can't ride, I'm not sure what protection we will be able to afford you. I assure you, you'll be quite safe riding with me."

Renya finally found her voice, and her soggy brain caught up. "No, I can travel. But why should I go with you?"

The man sighed again and rubbed his temples. He was younger than Renya initially thought, perhaps around her age. "I'm sorry. I know this must all be overwhelming for you, but we do not have the luxury of time. If you are fit to travel, we can converse along the way. But first, you are going to need some warmer clothes,

I think."

Renya pushed herself off the furs and stood. Quickly, as though he anticipated her movements, her would-be-rescuer rose to his feet. She swayed unsteadily, and he reached out with remarkable speed and steadied her. She fell into his chest and the masculine smell of the woods assaulted her nose again. He helped her back upright, made sure she was stable on her legs, his arms lingering on her hips for just a split second longer than they needed to. He withdrew them quickly and then cleared his throat again.

"We have little in the way of women's attire, but my manservant scoured the camp and found what we could for you. Unfortunately, we don't have a lady to attend to you. I'll stand guard outside as you change." He motioned to a small pile of clothing alongside the trunk and then swept out of the tent.

Renya took the opportunity of solitude to peek outside of the tent. The tall man had his back turned to the flap of the tent and stood tall and sentinel. She looked around the rest of the camp and saw men packing up and readying for travel. Wait...not men. Her keen eyes saw the sharp point of their ears and knew instantly she was not among her own kind. She should be scared, but what choices did she have available to her? She nearly died of exposure, and this man saved her.

She scurried back to the center of the tent and shrugged off her damp clothes before the man could come back in. She struggled into the pair of worn wool trousers and a loose fitting top. A silver cape made of the softest fur she had ever felt rested upon her shoulders, fastened with a silver pin. It was the same one the man wore, and it looked to be a perfect miniature of the strange animal she had seen when she first arrived, munching on the strange white roots. She knew the cape belonged to the man; the second she slipped it over her shoulders she was enveloped in his rich scent. Renya looked around for her boots, and found them by the fire, completely dry. She sighed in relief and slipped them on. She didn't trust this man, but she knew once she had a chance, she could escape and find her way home. However, she knew she would need dry clothes for any plan she came up with. It would be prudent to rest a bit and get a better sense of the land before trying to strike off on her own.

A moment later, the man called in. "Are you decent?" He didn't wait for a response before lifting the flap and sliding in. She yelled in protest, but his eyes were clamped shut. He looked absurd in the middle of his own tent, with his eyes squeezed shut. If she hadn't felt so unbalanced, she would have laughed at the scene.

"I'm dressed and warm, thanks to you." She figured she might as well acknowledge the hospitality he had shown her, even if she wasn't sure why he did so. Renya's experience with men reminded her that little was ever done without expecting something in return.

The man opened his eyes and looked at her. His gaze went to her face and then trailed along her loose shirt and up and down her legs. At once, she felt naked under his gaze and a hint of redness flushed up her neck and into her cheeks. Her heart thumped as if her suspicions had been confirmed and she knew exactly what he wanted from her. However, almost as if she imagined his intense scrutiny, his eyes bore back into hers and he nodded approval.

"If you'll come with me, please," he commanded

formally, and offered out his arm. She grabbed it, not because of his chivalrous offer, but because she was still unsure of her footing. Arm in arm, Renya followed him out of the tent into the cold, formidable land.

Her eyes adjusted to the bright light, and she looked around at her surroundings. Over two dozen men stared back at her, no doubt curious about the strange woman their lord had found helpless in the woods. She stared right back, not with hostility but with a look she hoped conveyed she was no damsel in distress. Once she passed by them, the men quickly got back to work, dousing fires and collapsing tents.

The man with the emerald eyes led her over to an enormous horse, larger than any Renya had ever seen. The mare's coat practically sparkled under the rising sun, and silver streaks shot off in every direction as the light danced along the fine, silken hairs. Her rescuer gave the horse an affectionate pat on the nose and a careful stroke up and down her long neck. He looked into the horse's eyes and said something low under his breath Renya couldn't make out, but she didn't think it sounded like her native tongue. She knew she was in a camp full of unknown men (or the like, since she still wasn't sure what they were) but the man's care and sensitivity to the animal comforted her for the moment.

The man's attention drew back to Renya, and he reached out to take her hand. "I apologize. I don't even know what your name is."

She looked up at him, his height making it difficult to catch his eyes. "I'm Renya," she said simply.

She thought she saw a flicker of something, perhaps confusion or maybe just unfamiliarity at the sounds in her name, as he placed a soft kiss on the back of her hand and lifted her onto the silver mare as if she weighed nothing. In an instant, he was behind her, nudging her slightly forward and making room for both of them in the pale leather saddle. It had no stirrups, and she had no idea how he swifty managed to climb up without them.

"Are you a sure rider?" he asked her, sensing her discomfort and tension.

"I've never been on a horse before..." she said, a bit taken back by the large animal between her thighs and its masculine rider, warm against her back.

"Don't worry, you are safe with me, Renya," he said. Her name sounded beautiful on his lips, almost like a lover's whisper. She had never heard her name spoken so sensually before. She wasn't sure if it was just the richness of his voice or if she imagined it. The man grabbed the horse's reins and called something out to his men. This time, Renya was sure it was an unfamiliar language.

At once, the silver horse gracefully took off in a quick sprint and the snowy terrain flew by. Renya yelped in surprise at the sudden speed which pushed her back into the man's solid chest. He chuckled at her reaction, and encircled one arm firmly against her waist, fingers splayed across her abdomen, while the other hand held the reins tight.

Renya tried to keep her body upright and away from his torso, but it was a losing battle as the powerful horse rounded a bank and leapt over a fallen tree. She made a sudden yip, and this time the man laughed aloud.

She recovered quickly and leaned back to ask him a question. "What is her name?"

"Starlia," he replied, his voice and breath warm

against her ear, and she shivered as if it hit her spine as well. "It means full of life."

"She's gorgeous," Renya replied. "But what am I to call you?"

A soft smile played on his lips, almost as though he was in some kind of internal struggle.

"You, my Little Fawn, may call me Grayden."

Chapter Ten

Grayden's mind whirled as Starlia sprinted faster along the worn trail. Renya. Her name was Renya? Given her unfamiliarity with his native language, he guessed she didn't know the meaning of her own name. Renya. *She who brings the light.* It couldn't be a coincidence, could it? While she wasn't Fae, she clearly had the mark of magic on her and a name passed down from the ancient Sun Realm. Fates, what did this mean?

His mind kept darting around all the possibilities as their progress continued. He was so distracted he almost forgot the object of his musings until he felt her body soften and relax against him and her shoulders slump. A smile relaxed his tight lips. She'd fallen asleep in the protective circle of his arms. He couldn't help but notice the way her full lips parted as she breathed and the way her chest rose and fell against him. Although her tunic was loose fitting, he could just make out the swell of her breasts. Her thighs were strong and shapely, but he quickly tore his gaze away. It was improper to stare at her while she was asleep against him. Yet the top of her head rested comfortably under his chin and the smell of her body so near him was intoxicating. Grayden felt his own body begin to respond uncontrollably to her nearness. He was a male, first and foremost. How long had passed since he had been with a woman? Or even been this close to one? He struggled to remember. Ruling the kingdom and keeping the shadows out of his ancestral lands was his priority and took up all of his time. During his early youth, he was a virile young prince, eager to enjoy life. He enjoyed his share of dalliances, but the stage didn't even last long enough to really sow his wild oats before he was forced into ruling. Now, Grayden was crushed under the weight of his responsibilities. They aged him considerably in the past five years and he was careful not to pursue anything but what was best for his lands. From sun up, until sundown, he worked in his chambers, consulted with his advisors, rode out into the land, and ran his lodge smoothly. The only regular release he had was when he sparred on the field with Phillippe.

Phillippe. His face flushed with guilt and he directed his thoughts on more honorable things, rather than the human woman resting peacefully against his chest, temporarily comforted in his arms.

He needed to find his brother and their men. He gently shifted Renya away from his lap and she stirred a bit, only to move back against his warm body, defeating the purpose of his moving her.

Charly noticed the girl was asleep and sped up to ride alongside Grayden.

"I'd say we've an hour left until we reach the border, my lord." He glanced at Renya's still form. "What have you learned about her?"

Grayden once again felt a strange wave of possessiveness creep over him. How dare Charly ask about her? What did he want with her? Grayden, after all, was the one to find her. He stopped himself and quickly pushed the instinct down and debated how much information to share.

"I think she came from the human realm, but

that's about all I've learned. She fell asleep pretty quickly once Starlia hit a steady pace. Travel through portals can be quite taxing, especially for humans with no magic. Oh, and her name is Renya." Grayden felt a pang of guilt for withholding the information about her mark and her name's meaning. It was an old name, most likely forgotten by those not descended from the first bloods. But until he figured out what this meant, he kept his thoughts to himself.

Charly nodded and rode alongside Grayden in silence, his copper-colored stallion struggling to keep up with Starlia's grueling pace.

Suddenly, Starlia reared up and Grayden struggled to keep her still. Renya woke up with a start.

"What's going on?" she asked, her eyes frantically darting around. Grayden could see the mistrust and alarm on her face. He wasn't sure what happened to her in the past, but she was extremely cautious around him.

"It's Phillippe. Or at least his horse, Necteria. Starlia's sister. She can sense her." Grayden patted Starlia comfortingly and urged her on. She trotted quickly through the tangle of thick woods, moving intentionally towards something that neither one could see. They broke into a clearing, and Grayden finally saw Necteria bolting towards them, carrying something dark along her back and bleeding from her side. Grayden felt Renya push herself further back into his body for protection as they slowed down to meet the rogue horse. He could feel Renya's heartbeat pick up and could practically smell the fear radiating off of her.

Grayden dismounted and then pulled Renya down from the horse and quickly put his body between her and the frightened mare. As Necteria approached, Grayden could see a figure draped across her wide back. He drew his sword, only to push it back into its sheath when he recognized his unconscious brother.

"Thank the Fates!" Grayden cried, running to his brother. He motioned for Charly to stay with Renya. Dimitri caught up, dismounted, and ran to the injured man, his robes swishing and dragging in the heavy snow. Grayden pulled Phillippe from Necteria's back and assessed him for injuries. His head was bleeding, matting his dark hair, and it appeared his arm was broken and perhaps a few ribs. His side was bleeding as well, and what he had mistaken for blood from Necteria's injury was actually from Phillippe. He was losing blood fast. Gods, what happened to him? Where were the rest of his men? If only Grayden's magic was stronger, he could at least stop the bleeding. He concentrated, but he felt the weakness of his power and nothing came forward. He was a shell of himself; his magic was completely depleted from overuse in the past weeks.

Grayden nodded to Charly, and he leaped onto the back of his horse and rode hard in the direction Necteria came from to find out what happened at the border.

Dimitri kneeled next to Grayden and Phillippe. "We need to get somewhere safe, and I need water and a fire. Eileen's inn is just a few miles from here, back at Chesterly."

Without a word, Grayden helped secure Phillippe to Dimitri's horse and ordered him to ride ahead. Grayden sent another one of his men after Charly to assess the damage from the fray and to let Charly know where they were heading. He glanced over at Renya, her eyes wide as she took in the extent of Phillippe's injuries. Her fingers moved as if she longed to help, but didn't know what to do.

Grayden strode over to her and offered his hand. Renya grasped it, obviously afraid of what she'd seen, and followed him to Starlia. He lifted her up on the mare's back and settled in behind her again. His arousal long gone, he gnashed his teeth in worry.

"Is he your brother?" Renya asked quietly, tilting her head back towards Grayden as Starlia raced after Dimitri's horse.

"Yes." He looked down at her and he could see the sorrow on her face. He suppressed an urge to hug her closer to him, seeking comfort in her arms. He hadn't sought comfort in the arms of a woman since his mother's death. What was it about this woman?

"I'm so sorry," Renya said softly, and he watched as her long lashes dipped downward. Grayden had the sudden urge to bring his hand to her face and stroke her freezing skin, but he fought against it. "What happened?"

"I'm not sure. He and our troops were patrolling our borders, and the men were attacked."

"Attacked by what?" she asked.

"Not what, but who," he said, and he was sure Renya could pick up on the audible despair in his voice, but he couldn't hid it. "The Shadow Queen is seeking power from all corners of the realms. She has a seer in her command who has foretold of a power source unlike no other somewhere within our world, and she will stop at nothing to find it. She won't be happy until she alone rules the realms."

"Power?" Renya asked. "Like magic?" Her eyebrows raised in disbelief and Grayden saw awe and perhaps a little fear in her expression.

"Exactly like magic, Little Fawn," Grayden

answered, watching the thoughtful look on Renya's face.

"Do you have magic? Can you ask a person that, or is it considered rude?"

If the situation with his brother wasn't so dire, he would have laughed. "No, Renya. It's not rude. And to answer your question, yes. I possess some degree of magic."

"Can you use magic to open a door?"

He knew what she was getting at, and he sighed. "You mean a portal? Perhaps, but it would require strength I don't currently possess and would leave my magic spent for weeks, perhaps even months. And I don't know which human portal you traveled through, and it could be dangerous to open a portal, not knowing where in time and space you arrived from. The safest way to send someone back through a portal is by having someone on the other side first open it."

Her lip trembled, and Grayden felt guilty for his honesty. It wasn't in his character to lie, but he hated being the cause of her quivering bottom lip. Perhaps he should have given her some false hope. He wondered what she left behind in the human world that gave her such pain to leave behind. He found himself hoping it wasn't a man, and he felt foolish the second the thought crossed his mind. What was wrong with him? He knew the girl all but a few hours. There were plenty of women trying to gain his favor and attention, but he never paid them the slightest bother, much to their disappointment and irritation. Most women who lusted after him sought him out because of his magic, hoping to sire talented offspring and further their own positions and status. He cared not for the superficial women who came to seek attention at his court. After realizing that his interest was everywhere but these girls, they ceased coming altogether. Grayden suspected it was Tumwalt trying to arrange a match for him, hoping he would fall in love with a girl hand-picked by his advisors.

"You know where I came from? And that I'm human?"

"I surmised as much, yes." Grayden looked down at her face as a tear slowly fell from one of her icy blue eyes. He reached down and wiped it gently from her cheek before it froze. Her face flushed, perhaps from his touch, or perhaps from the embarrassment of crying in front of a stranger. He felt a tenderness towards her that he didn't think he had ever felt before.

"If you're not human, what are you?" She looked at him, scrutinizing his features.

"You are in the Fae realm, Little Fawn."

Renya opened her mouth as if to ask another question, but Grayden drew her attention ahead to the tiny inn. She nodded, seeming to understand the rest of their conversation would have to wait.

Chapter Eleven

T hey approached the inn, and Renya sat up a little straighter as Grayden pulled back the reins on his horse, slowing her slightly before he dismounted. His feet barely hit the ground before he pulled Renya off and lowered her down. Renya swayed on her feet, but for the first time in a while she felt grounded enough to trust her own footing.

Grayden motioned for her to follow him, and they approached the stone door of the inn and pushed inside. The warmth of the building instantly hit Renya, and she rubbed her chilled hands together as she looked around. It was bigger inside than it looked, and there was a stone hearth holding a roaring fire against one wall, and the tables and chairs in the closest proximity to the fire were full of patrons, sipping the contents of their large, pewter mugs and talking loudly. A hush fell over the room as they entered, and the men stopped what they were doing and bowed their heads respectfully.

As eyes turned away from Grayden and towards Renya, he once again placed his body between her and the other people in the room. Renya was puzzled. Was his world so dangerous that every interaction required protection?

Grayden called to a short woman with a plump, round face and a worn green dress with an apron covering the front. He spoke to her in a low tone while

Renya looked around the room, observing.

"This is Eileen," he told Renya, motioning for the woman to step forward. She gave a little curtsy and bobbed her head. "She will take you to a room and see to your needs. I must check in on my brother. You will be quite safe, I promise you. I'll be a few doors down." He gave her a slight bow of his head, and Renya could hear his boots thumping on the stairs as he took them two at a time.

"If you'll follow me, mistress," said the woman in a friendly, comforting tone. "I'll put you next to the prince's room. I imagine you'll stay a while until Prince Phillippe recovers enough to travel." Renya followed Eileen up the stairs and towards a room at the end of the hall. She couldn't see where Grayden had gone, but guessed that his brother was in one of the other rooms.

Eileen opened the door and Renya stepped inside. A small fireplace was in the corner, lighting up the tiny room. A simple bed, table and chair made up the furniture. After being out in the cold for almost two days, it was a welcome sight. Renya moved towards the bed and sat down. It creaked slightly under her weight, but she didn't care. She was suddenly so tired.

"My daughter, Sari, will be in soon with a hot pitcher of water, some suitable clothes for you, and something to eat," Eileen said as she started to close the door.

"Oh, what I'm wearing is fine," Renya insisted. She was planning on stripping down bare and sliding under the covers while her clothing dried by the fire.

"Nonsense," replied Eileen, opening the door again. "His Lordship expects you to be seen to properly. I'm sure you've scandalized his men enough."

Renya scoffed. Scandalized the men? She was fully clothed. She didn't feel any need to change. However... Grayden saved her when she was near death and refusing any kindness seemed imprudent. She'd wondered why he helped her so much this far. Was it the way of his people? Did he expect something from her in return? She shuddered, thinking of the things the senator wanted in return for his help. She'd learned the hard way that people, men in particular, rarely did things without expecting something in return. Grayden seemed gentle and kind, but then again, so did the senator. He listened to her lofty, naïve ideals and nodded, all the while knowing he would never really help her unless she gave him what he wanted.

"Who are his men?" Renya asked, finally hoping to get some answers about the strange men she found herself in the company of.

"Soldiers, loyal to the Snowden line," Eileen explained.

"What's the Snowden line?"

"His Lordship's family line. It traces back to the beginning, when the elements and seasons all had balance and their own power. Over the last thousand years, changes throughout our land have occurred, and in the last few hundred, it's been for the worse. Our world is changing, and too quickly. There used to be realms for every season and elemental position, but over the last millennium some of the greatest houses have fallen. We've lost the Star Realm, the Sun Realm, and the Equinox Kingdom, just to name a few."

Renya urged her to keep going, trying to gather all the information she could, a habit from her years in journalism. "What happened? Why did the houses fall?"

Eileen looked at her, wondering if her curiosity was sincere. "Magic. Or lack thereof. Everyone has a theory, but one Fae's guess is as good as another's. Some folk think that as more and more portals opened and trade across other worlds became possible, bloodlines became mixed and diluted. More and more babes were born without magic. What used to be the norm is now the rare exception. Other folk think there's a deeper, darker power holding the kingdom in shadow. That's what your handsome young prince thinks."

"He is not my prince," Renya snorted. Whoever this man was, he was just a stranger. Sure, she found him attractive, but with his muscular build and handsome features, she was sure any woman would.

Eileen looked at her squarely. "You sure about that? He went through an awful lot of trouble to get you here safe, especially when his brother's life was on the line. Never were any brothers closer than the Snowden boys. Yet Dimitri told me Prince Grayden delayed leaving camp for four hours while you recovered, all the while his brother's life was in danger. Mark my words, girl, he finds something special in you. Best find out what it is and soon, or head back to whatever land you hail from."

A young girl, perhaps Renya's age, appeared in the doorway next to Eileen and entered the room with a steaming pitcher and basin, some white linens draped over her arm, and a plate of food. Her clothes were tidy and her auburn hair was braided down her back and secured with a ribbon. She had an oval-shaped face and large, caramel-colored eyes. The girl set the pitcher and basin on the small table, and then moved towards Renya, handing her a soft white cloth and what appeared to be a clean linen nightdress. Eileen seized the opportunity of her daughter's arrival to step out the door before Renya could pepper her with more questions, her feet falling heavy on the stairs.

"My name is Sari," the girl said, curtsying, but not before Renya tried to stop her.

"You don't need to do that. I'm just a regular person."

Sari stared at her. "You travel with His Lordship," she said simply. Sari set the tray of food on the table and backed out of the room before Renya could ask her anything.

For the first time since waking up in Grayden's tent, Renya was alone. She was glad for the opportunity to collect her thoughts and try to strategize and think through her current situation. But first, she desperately wanted to get clean. Her hair felt ashy from the smoke of the fire and her face was salty from her tears. She went over to the pitcher and poured the water in the basin. The water steamed, and she dipped the towel in the hot water. She washed herself carefully, shucking off her borrowed wet clothes and placing them in front of the fire, and then she pulled the nightdress over her head. It was simple, but comfortable with a blue ribbon tying at the neck. Her bare feet traveled over to the wooden table and she looked down at the plate of food. There were hunks of a dark-colored bread, some kind of strange fruit shaped into stars and simple farmer's cheese. Renya devoured them ravenously, hardly tasting anything as she swallowed. She hadn't had a proper meal for weeks, even before she came to this strange land. Her finances at home didn't allow for much in the way of meals, and she survived mainly on popcorn and dried fruit. Her aunt cooked the last warm meal she had, right before Renya left for

Seattle. Oh, how she missed her aunt. She pictured her as she had been then, fluttering around the kitchen and chopping vegetables while still trying to persuade Renya to stay in California.

With her belly full, Renya crawled into the bed. She didn't think another bed had ever looked as inviting as she pulled the coverlet up to her chin. Strategizing and figuring out how to get home would have to wait until tomorrow, she thought as her head hit the pillow and she quickly fell asleep.

Chapter Twelve

"Thank the Fates he got to us when he did," Dimitri said, as he tied off the last stitch he had placed alongside the back of Phillippe's head. He dropped the needle into a basin and wiped his hands on a clean cloth. "If he would have lost any more blood, the Snowden brothers would be no more."

Grayden sighed thankfully, fully exhaling for the first time in days. His brother was safe. But as for his men...Charly had returned with several dozen wounded soldiers and a makeshift infirmary had been set up at the inn. They'd lost at least ten dozen back at the field, according to Charly's rough count. Grayden still needed to interview the men well enough to speak, but his brother was his first priority. Family first, strategy second.

He clapped Dimitri on the shoulder. "Your help will be well rewarded, my friend. I appreciate the care you provided to my brother. If it had been anyone but you, I don't think he would have made it," Grayden said sincerely, "and I also thank you for the discretion involving our earlier conversations about Renya."

"There is no need to thank me for either," the healer said. "I served your father well, and I will continue my loyalty to the Snowden line."

Grayden nodded his thanks. Talk like that still embarrassed him. He sometimes felt like an imposter in his father's place, as if he was just playing king for the day and his father would return at any moment and rescue him from the job.

Grayden turned to his brother and surveyed the damage. Despite being unconscious and deathly pale, he looked much better after being cleaned up a bit. Dimitri had set his arm and wrapped his ribs. Phillippe had two lacerations needing to be stitched along his brow and the base of his scalp, but the worst injury was the wound at his side. It took Dimitri almost an hour to close it, and he was still concerned and watching it closely. "Dark magic touched him here," was all the healer said.

Grayden sat down next to his brother on the bed, his weight sinking it slightly. He wished Phillippe was conscious so they could discuss the attack. And Renya. He knew the girl was something important. He hadn't heard of anyone traveling through a portal in the Snow Lands in over a hundred years. Yet she was human. Did she have a part to play in restoring the balance to their world? He needed answers, but he knew he wouldn't get them sitting on his brother's bed. Grayden glanced at Phillippe's chest and watched it rise and fall. Once Grayden was satisfied Phillippe was going to be okay, he headed out of the room. He hesitated at the door he asked Eileen to put Renya in, but decided against disturbing the exhausted young woman. Traveling through the portal seemed to have taken a lot out of her, and combined with almost dying from exposure, she needed to recuperate as well. Besides, he needed to talk to his soldiers and get to the bottom of what happened on that battlefield. The mystery of the pretty, blue-eyed human would have to wait.

Grayden walked down the hall and eyed the

makeshift surgery set up in the available rooms. He'd have to talk to Eileen about giving up his room to make space for the men. Tables were cleared and brought in to maximize the space, holding men with varying degrees of injury, and several healers from around the area were called in to assist Dimitri. Those who were able were assisting the healers. Grayden's heart sank as he glanced into the rooms. These injuries were grave. It appeared the Shadow Queen had amassed a larger army than he originally deduced. Where was Sion? He hoped nothing had befallen him. Without Sion's eyes and ears inside Queen Cressida's court, Grayden was blind to attacks like this. This was the longest they went without information from him. He knew Sion planned to get closer to the queen and find a place in her innermost circle, but Grayden was now worried that it had been too risky.

Grayden took his eyes off the wounded men before him as Charly approached. He hadn't had a second to catch up with him. Charly's eyes were dark and frantic, and a knot formed in Grayden's stomach. Whatever he had to say was worrisome, indeed.

"My lord, may I suggest we head to your room and talk in private?"

Grayden led the way back down the hall. He passed Renya's room and thought again of the girl. Fates, he was possessed. It must be the mystery of her and what she could mean for the kingdom that drew him to her. They hardly had any interaction at all, yet he couldn't help but think of her.

They entered Grayden's room and sat down at the small table. Charly looked around the room, obviously not eager to deliver the news he bore. Grayden knew Charly's father, who had trained Phillippe. After Charly's father had died, Charly joined their forces to help support his mother and his younger sister. Grayden respected him highly for that fact alone, regardless of his skill with a blade and his loyalty.

"Out with it, Charly," Grayden commanded, as he poured them both a large mug of fireale from the jug on the table. He had a feeling they both were going to need it and hopefully it would help loosen Charly's tongue.

"It's bad, my lord. I followed Necteria's tracks back to the edge of the border. It appeared the battle took place on both sides of the river, both on our lands and the lands seized by the Shadow Queen."

Grayden frowned. His soldiers knew better than to cross the river and leave their territory. He knew Charly was aware of the fact, too. "Why would they cross?" he asked, slightly angry at the thought of his men provoking this attack and weakening their army. He knew Phillippe wouldn't take chances like that either. Something didn't make sense.

"That's just it, my lord. I don't think they did. There were only...pieces of our men on the other side of the river."

The color drained from Grayden's face. Pieces of his men? What in the Gods' name had happened?

Charly continued, staring into his untouched mug, his fingers lacing and unlacing nervously in his lap. "I saw minor damage done to the other side, only one or two dozen fallen Shadow Realm soldiers. I'm afraid this was the work of...dragons."

Instantly, Grayden pictured the wound on his brother's side. Dragons. Sweet Fates. No wonder Dimitri struggled with closing it and staunching the bleeding. But how was it possible? How were dragons in their world? They didn't belong in any of the lands here. He shuddered as he tried to envision the portal Cressida must have opened to bring them here. He couldn't even manage to open a small portal to send Renya back to her own land, yet the Shadow Queen had gained so much power she could bring these beasts into their world? This was the worst news he could have gotten. He knew he was fighting an uphill battle to restore any type of balance to their world, but for the first time, he seriously now doubted the possibility he would succeed. He had never felt so helpless before. The real war hadn't even started and he already failed his people. Grayden was no closer to restoring the magic and lands of the realm than his father had been. For the first time in a while, he wished his father were here. He wanted someone else to shoulder the responsibility. The weight of the kingdom's problems practically crushed him over the past few years. He often felt hollow inside, like beyond the crown and his kingdom, there was nothing else left of him. There were no delights left for him, and he had nothing else to offer. Grayden knew he carried the bulk of the burden for his elder brother. Part of it was because of his brother's lack of magic, and the other half was because that was just how Grayden was. Unselfish in all things, loyal, righteous and dutiful. His mother had raised him well, but with his boyhood ending so abruptly, there was hardly time for him to come into himself.

He never needed to wear a crown upon his head, because he had become it.

Chapter Thirteen

B y the time Renya awoke, it was nightfall. She woke up thirsty and hungry beyond belief. Renya crept slowly out of bed and stretched her muscles. She was tense and sore everywhere. Between walking in snow drifts and riding for hours, there wasn't any part of her body that didn't ache. Muscles she didn't know she had burned from use. Her thighs were red and chaffed from riding. She hoped they'd spend a few days here at the inn; she didn't think she could get back on another horse anytime soon.

Renya searched the small room for something else to eat or drink. She was hoping Eileen or Sari might have left something. What time was it? She looked out the small window next to the fireplace, but all she could see was snow and darkness. The panes of the window bore frost on the outside and condensation on the inside. She shivered and moved closer to the fireplace to warm her hands. Renya stood there for a few minutes until her thirst drove her out of her room in search of something to drink. She looked around the tiny room for something to cover her nightgown with, but the clothes she strategically placed to dry by the fire had disappeared entirely. She felt it must have been the work of Eileen, terrified that she would insist upon wearing them again. Renya debated taking the coverlet off the bed to use as a robe, but decided against it. She pushed open the door quietly. Eileen said Grayden's room was next to hers, but she didn't want to disturb him. She walked past the other rooms. Some doors were closed, some were open. Renya peaked inside one room as she passed and saw the same man who had ridden with them, the one in black robes, assisting a man sitting up. They must be using the rooms as a makeshift hospital. Renya felt guilty at once for having a room to herself. She'd have to speak to someone about the situation. Renya continued down the hall, unseen. She guessed it was very late, given the lack of noise she heard, outside of the whispered voices of the healers. Renya descended the stairs, barefoot.

She was right in her assumption. The main room, previously full of patrons, was now empty, save for one lone man in the corner, passed out with a mug of something dark next to him. By the looks of it, he was sleeping off one hell of a hangover. Every world has their vices, Renya thought to herself.

She crept past the bearded man and headed for a door off the main room. She guessed it would be a kitchen. Renya was hoping for just some water; after seeing the man unconscious at his table, she didn't think partaking in whatever he had been having was a good idea.

Renya pushed the door open, and sure enough, a small kitchen greeted her. She could barely see the top of a large fireplace behind a rectangular table. Nearest to the door, a tall wooden box stood. It felt colder the closer Renya inched towards it, and she was thrilled when she opened it to find blocks of ice keeping food and beverages cold. She saw several large jugs of different colored liquids and grabbed a few. She would have to use some trial and error to figure out which ones would not leave her inebriated. That's all she needed in an inn full of strange men in a strange world.

She moved toward the long cooking bench nearest the fire to search for a glass. There was a short shelf underneath, and she found a large gray mug. She set it on the table and went for the cranberry colored jug first. The others were various colors of amber, which she assumed would most likely be some kind of beer or ale. She poured the tiniest amount of the reddish liquid into the mug and lifted it towards her mouth, trying to pick up a smell as the liquid ran towards her mouth.

"I wouldn't do that if I were you."

Renya let out a small shriek and nearly dropped the mug. The voice came from below her. She looked down and sprawled in front of the fire on top of his fur cloak was Grayden. His tunic was off, and he was bare-chested with one arm resting behind his head. His legs crossed at the ankle, and he still wore his black knee-high boots. He'd removed his belt, and his dark pants hung dangerously low on the hollow parts of his hips. His other hand was resting lazily over his flat stomach. Renya gulped and her face flushed red.

"I...what?" she stammered, trying to take her eyes off the muscular planes of his chest. Every part of him was well-defined. It was apparent from his physique that he engaged in strenuous types of exercise daily.

He grinned a boyish grin, almost as though he could tell she was staring at him and embarrassed by it. "The drink you just poured," he said, green eyes sparkling. "It's fireale. With a woman your size and with no tolerance to it, it'll have you speaking nonsense before it even hits your belly."

"Oh, thanks," Renya squealed, trying to look at

anything besides the half-naked man on the floor. She settled on staring intently at the jug full of fireale and went to put the stopper back in the jug's neck.

In a flash, Grayden's hand covered hers and his voice came from behind her, dangerously close. His other hand reached around her body and rested on the table. She was completely circled in his arms, his bare chest against her back, her head under his chin. Renya could feel the heat radiating from his body behind her, and the spots on her neck seemed to warm in response. Her body tingled in a way that had nothing to do with the scorching fireplace.

"Leave it. Now that you've opened it, I'll take some. And I'll find you something more suitable to drink," Grayden said, dropping her hand and strolling towards the icebox. Her hand felt hot, even though he had only held it for a split second. Renya admired his strong back as he walked. His upper arms were muscular, and she tried not to stare. She was always someone who preferred the inside of a person to the outside, but she had to admit he was incredibly attractive. Under the thick winter clothing he wore, it was impossible to see just how sculpted and perfect his body was. But now, stripped down, it was easy to see the definition of his arms and chest. He had narrow hips, but broad shoulders and muscular legs. A ragged scar traced the line of his scapula and Renya wondered what had happened. Although it marred his skin, she found it only added to his handsomeness.

She watched him shuffle around and bring out a peach-colored drink. "Lotus Apple," he said, crossing to the opposite side of the table and pulling out another mug. He poured a fresh glass of the fizzy beverage and passed it across to her. Grayden grabbed the mug she had filled with the fireale and poured some more of the ale in. He lifted the mug slightly. "To you, Renya."

She blushed, but lifted her glass. She brought it to her lips and took a small sip. Instantly, her taste buds tingled with delight. It was sweet, yet earthy, and amazingly refreshing. She let out a small, happy sigh. Grayden's eyes drifted to her lips for a few seconds before shifting back up to her eyes.

"Good?" he asked her.

"It's...amazing. Like nothing I've ever tasted before," she said as she took another drink.

"I thought you'd enjoy it. When I was little, my mother used to take me to pick lotus apples. We have a large orchard, and we'd spend the entire day picking buckets and buckets full. Then we'd spread out a blanket and eat some of our spoils," he smiled somewhat sadly. "It's been a long time since I thought about those times."

Renya caught the tone of his voice. "She's gone, isn't she?" She knew the answer before he responded.

"Yes. Five years now. Both her and my father. They came down with an unknown illness. Healer after healer came, but no one knew what it was. The worst thing...they kept us away from them. Without knowing the cause, my father's advisors worried about the line of succession..." he drifted off, staring past Renya and out the window.

Without thinking, Renya reached across the table and took Grayden's hand. Again, she felt the warmth there, as if his body ran a few degrees warmer. He stared at her hand on top of his, then looked back up at her, his face unreadable. She smiled somewhat uncomfortably. Touching a man like this...it brought back memories that she didn't wish to address.

"I get it. I lost both my parents, too. They died shortly after I was born. A car accident. I don't remember them at all, obviously. My Aunt Agatha raised me. She was —is—good to me. It was lonely, though. But sometimes I get...I don't know, this feeling of them? Like a warmness in my chest, almost like they are still here."

She looked up at him and saw a look of curiosity in his eyes. She thought he was going to ask her more, to elaborate on her confession, but he just squeezed her hand. His calloused thumb brushed her knuckle, and a bolt of electricity coursed down her spine. Renya attempted to steady her breathing at his touch, deciding if she wanted to pull away or see the comfort through.

The door suddenly opened, and Eileen bristled in, carrying a bundle of wood. Grayden removed his hand from Renya's quickly, breaking the connection, and casually took a drink of his ale as if the moment never happened.

"Mistress, what are you doing here in the kitchen?" she asked. "It's the middle of the night! And in your nightshirt, of all things! And in front of His Lordship!"

Renya crossed her arms in front of her chest. "I'm completely covered," she said, exasperated.

Grayden laughed. The sound was so rich that both women couldn't help but smile at the charming sound. "Don't worry, Eileen. I'm nothing if not an honorable man."

Eileen rolled her eyes and stared at both of them, then hurried to the other side of the table where Renya stood and tossed more wood in the fire. "I see you've made a bed for yourself over here."

"I couldn't sleep in a soft bed knowing men who

suffered in my name were in pain. They need it more than I do."

Eileen didn't seem to have a response or argument for that. Renya added his statement to her list of things she was learning about him. Almost as though there was a formula she could use in order to decide if he was trustworthy, she kept the list in the forefront of her mind.

Eileen finished up with the fire and then made her way to the door. Before she left, she gave Renya a sharp look. "Sari will be up to dress you in the morning. Please wait for her before you go gallivanting about in your underthings."

Renya scoffed as Grayden chuckled again. The sound of his laugh was welcoming and warm. Renya dropped her scowl and laughed, too.

She decided now was a good time to broach the subject of her room as well. "I wasn't sure who to ask, but I also wanted to talk to someone about my bedroom situation. I don't feel comfortable taking up an entire room to myself while there are injured men sleeping on tables."

"Absolutely not," Grayden replied, the sternness in his tone surprising Renya. "You are under my care and charge and you will be in your own room, where I can ensure no one bothers you."

"But—"

"It's not up for discussion," he said, finishing his ale and slamming the mug down harder than he meant to.

Green eyes met blue ones as they glared at each other. Renya wanted to argue, but she also didn't know this man and didn't want to push him. Yet, she wasn't the type of woman to take no for an answer. She held his gaze, not backing down from the intense scrutiny of his eyes.

Finally, Grayden broke the tension, letting out a deep sigh that seemed to echo in the room. "Renya, I'm sorry. I just...want you safe."

"But why? I'm just a stranger you met on the road. For all you know, I could be dangerous."

Grayden's upper lip twitched. She could tell he was trying his hardest not to laugh at her. She glowered at him. He lifted his hands up in mock defeat.

"Yes, you're very terrifying, all angry and pink-faced in your nightdress," he laughed.

She wanted to argue, but it felt too good to laugh with him. This situation she was in was scary and she knew she would be dead right now if it wasn't for this man. Perhaps another mark should go in the trustworthy column for that fact alone.

She sighed, knowing she'd lost the battle. But she was determined to win the war and get herself back home. If a few concessions were needed, she'd put up with it.

Grayden grabbed their empty mugs and put them in the farmhouse-style sink. He held out his arm to Renya, and she only hesitated slightly before grabbing it. She followed him out of the kitchen, past the unconscious man in the dining room, and back upstairs to the door outside her bedroom.

He pushed open the door for her and she scooted underneath his arm into the room.

Renya stood in the middle of the small space and looked at him. "Since you gave up your room and are insistent I keep this one, the least I can do is offer you a spot in front of the fire. I'm sure the floor here is equally uncomfortable, but at least Eileen won't step on you in the morning." She wasn't sure she wanted him to accept and her stomach clenched, wondering if she shouldn't have made the offer. Alone in a room with a strange man? Had she learned nothing?

He looked past her shoulder and into the cozy room. She could tell he was tempted by the way his face softened. But instead, he shook his head no and grabbed her hand. He bent his head down and placed a tender kiss on her knuckles.

"Sleep well, Little Fawn."

Chapter Fourteen

G rayden sat in front of the fire in the main room. He'd gone back to the kitchen and gathered up his things; he knew he wouldn't get any more rest tonight. Besides, with Charly finally relieved of his duty for the evening, there was no one else to watch the inn...and Renya. He worried about her appearance in this world and her survival. She was strong, but knew nothing about Fae and needed to learn fast.

A grin played on Grayden's lips as he thought of her in her nightdress, silently challenging him. She was so brave and full of life. When he saw her creep into the kitchen and pour herself a glass of fireale, Grayden was tempted to let her take just a sip. Despite his warning, if any female could handle fireale, it would probably be Renya.

He thought back to their conversation. Renya was orphaned as a child. He wondered if she possessed some Fae blood in her. That might explain why she was drawn to the portal, and why he seemed to be drawn to her. Since she didn't know her parents, it was possible one or both might have had some Fae in their lineage, maybe even descendents from the fallen Sun Realm. It wasn't unheard of for Fae to occasionally move to human realms. Usually, the ones possessing the smallest and weakest bits of magic could make it in the human world by doing tricks and putting on shows. Yet he doubted Renya's parents had been pulling various animals out of hats.

He watched the vermilion sunrise through the window before heading upstairs to check on his brother. He entered the room and was surprised to see Dimitri already at Phillippe's bedside.

"Dimitri, you need to sleep. There are other healers here now," Grayden said gently from the doorway.

"I will, my lord, but he's gaining consciousness. Look."

Grayden moved towards Phillippe's bed. Sure enough, his eyes fluttered open. Grayden's heart lightened considerably the moment he saw his brother's gray eyes attempting to focus in the dim light.

"Nice of you to join us, brother."

Phillippe tried to sit up, but Grayden lightly pushed him back towards the mattress.

"You need to rest. We almost lost you back there. We still might if you don't take it easy and listen for once."

Phillippe's eyes were frantic, and he whispered, "Dragons."

Grayden sighed. "I know, Phillippe. I know. Do you know how many?"

Phillippe closed his eyes as if visualizing the battlefield. "Three, maybe four," he croaked.

"We'll figure out a way to handle it. I just wish I knew what she was planning," Grayden replied, trying to sound hopeful but failing miserably.

Phillippe tried to sit up again before Dimitri halted him.

"Sion?" he asked, looking at both Dimitri and Grayden.

"No, he's gone silent. We'll have to figure out another way to infiltrate her court if we don't hear something soon. I won't lie to you. I'm worried about him," Grayden answered.

"He's...strong...he'll be...okay." His voice was cracked and scratchy.

Grayden grabbed a glass of water from the nightstand and raised it to Phillippe's lips. He drank deep, relief on his face.

"I hope he'll be okay. He's a good man, one of the best spies we've ever had. But...we have some other matters to discuss," Grayden said.

Dimitri took this as his cue to leave the brothers alone to talk. Black robes swishing, he left the room.

Phillippe looked at Grayden expectedly.

Grayden cleared his throat. "On the way to the southern borders, I came across a girl. A woman, actually —"

Phillippe groaned, both from pain and from his brother's words. "Please don't tell me you're trying to marry...me off. At least let my ribs heal before you push me into an arranged marriage."

Grayden glared, but continued his tale. "Like I said, I found a woman. She was unconscious and appeared to come from a human realm. She's also marked by Fae magic."

Phillippe looked astonished. "A portal?" he asked.

Grayden nodded. "Her name is Renya."

Phillippe raised his eyes and then grimaced from the slight movement. "Renya? You don't think..."

"That she's somehow linked to the Sun Realm? Perhaps linked to their prophecy? I'm beginning to wonder. She has no real recollection of her parents and was raised by an aunt in the human world. She obviously does not know who or what she might be. As soon as you're fit to travel, I want to take her back and have her meet with Almory."

"I think you need to leave sooner rather than later, brother," Phillippe said thoughtfully. "I doubt I'll be able to ride for at least a week and we shouldn't leave our gates unprotected for that long." Phillippe winced in pain but continued. "We're talking about dragons here, Grayden. Almory needs to know what we are dealing with now. We might need to put out a call for more men as well. If you can gather them, as soon as I'm able, I'll start their training."

Grayden nodded in agreement. "Wise counsel. I'll take Renya with me. I'd like Almory to examine her mark as soon as possible and see if he can pick up any clues about who she is and why she's here." Grayden looked down at his brother.

"Oh...and I know I haven't said it yet, but I'm really glad you're—"

"I know Grayden, I know," Phillippe said, before lying his head back on the pillow.

Grayden left the room and went in search of Charly. If he was going to leave straight away, he needed his second in command to watch over everything here at the inn. He found him in the next room over, talking to some soldiers. Charly saw Grayden and halted his conversation and approached Grayden.

"I'm going to head back to Snowden Lodge," he said. "I need to talk to Almory and start organizing our tactical forces."

Charly nodded. "What about Renya? Should I look after her?"

Another wave of protectiveness surged through Grayden, but he let the feeling pass over him and took a deep breath. "No, I'm going to take her with me."

At this, Charly looked puzzled. "Surely you don't mean to travel alone with her? My lord, I don't doubt you, but traveling alone with a female to protect during these times could be quite dangerous."

Grayden looked Charly straight in the eye. "Nothing—absolutely nothing—will harm her while she's with me."

Charly sensed the finality in Grayden's tone and gave a small nod of acceptance. Grayden stepped outside of the room and headed down the stairs to find Renya. He located her in the kitchen with Sari. Renya must have given in to Eileen because she wore a long purple dress with a laced bodice. Grayden imagined that it must have been quite the effort on Eileen's part to coerce Renya into the gown. Although her legs were now properly covered, he could just see the top of her chest. Honestly, women's fashions confused him. He couldn't look at her in the tight trousers she had on yesterday, but any man passing by would get a glance at her cleavage. Grayden caught himself growling at the thought. He wanted to take her away from this inn for reasons having nothing to do with getting her to Almory.

Renya looked up from the long table as he entered. Sari gave Grayden a quick curtsy and made an excuse to leave the kitchen. Grayden looked down at Renya. She had a dab of ground grain on her face and her hands were covered in a sticky dough, but a sweet smile lit up her face. He watched her work a dark-colored dough on the floured surface, before finally speaking.

"What are you doing?" he asked, raising an eyebrow.

Renya blushed. Grayden was starting to realize she

turned pink frequently in the face. He loved when she blushed in embarrassment. It made her seem so young and just a little vulnerable. He couldn't fathom why she was blushing now, though.

"I asked Sari to teach me how to make a pie," she started. "I wanted to thank you for assisting me with... everything. It's...a lotus apple pie."

His eyes softened as he looked down at her pink cheeks and pretty blue eyes. She seemed embarrassed to be making something for him. Based on her behavior, he gathered that in her world, boundary lines between males and females were more blurred, and a domestic act such as baking a pie must hold some kind of special meaning. No matter what it meant in her world, he knew it was a heartfelt gesture. He felt bad he wouldn't get to taste it after her hard work.

"That was thoughtful of you, Little Fawn. But I'm afraid we must depart within the hour."

"Leave?" Renya questioned. "So soon? Is something wrong? Is there danger?"

"I'm afraid being around me is a constant danger, Renya. But no, not immediate danger. Now that my brother has regained consciousness, I need to head home and see to things there."

"Oh, I'm so glad he's awake. I feel guilty for not asking earlier. How is he?"

"He's well enough to bark orders," he said with a smile. "I think he's going to be alright."

"I'm happy to hear it. So...you're taking me with you?" she asked, and he tried not to read any amount of hopefulness in her tone.

The thought of traveling alone with her made his heart beat a bit faster. He knew she must be sore and tired from the past few days, but something in him would not allow him to leave her behind. He refused her offer to stay in her room last night, but was unable to get her beautiful green eyes and sweet smile off his mind. The instant he turned down the offer to spend the night in her room, he regretted it. He wouldn't let her reputation be ruined like that, though, even if all he did was watch her sleep.

"Yes. You'll be the safest with me."

"I thought you just said being around you is dangerous," she said, a little smirk playing on her lips.

"Trust me, Little Fawn, anywhere in this land is dangerous, especially right now. But I swear to you, on my life, no harm shall come to you under my watch. You have my word."

Chapter Fifteen

Renya wanted to believe Grayden. Wanted to believe she was safe. But after her dealings in Los Angeles, she struggled to believe anyone had her best interests at heart. Except for Aunt Agatha. Her heart lurched. Her aunt. How long until she realized Renya was gone? She usually called her once a week. Renya imagined her waiting for the call that would never come. She'd probably call Renya with no success for a few days. At what point would she come up to Seattle? Go through her vacated apartment? Move her things out? Tears stung Renya's eyes as she imagined it.

"Renya, what's wrong?" Grayden asked, concerned.

"I'm just thinking of my aunt and what will happen when she realizes I'm gone. She has no one else."

Grayden sighed. "Renya, if there's a way to increase my powers and open a portal for you, I will. I can't guarantee anything, but I'll do whatever is in my power to see you home safely."

Renya looked into his wintergreen eyes. She saw honesty and truth in them. Maybe, just maybe...this man was decent. She nodded and gave him a tight smile. "Okay then, let's head out. Just give me a second to get my things together."

A half an hour later, Renya stood outside of the inn while Grayden went to fetch Starlia from the tiny stables.

The inn wasn't big enough to house them all, so the extra horses from the troops were grazing around the property.

Eileen and Sari had been busy packing some provisions for their journey and some extra clothes for Renya. They also found some warm gloves for her and a better pair of boots. She flexed her fingers in the leather gloves, grateful that she wouldn't endure the stinging sensation she experienced before.

Renya watched as Grayden brought Starlia over. She wasn't eager to get back in the saddle, but she was looking forward to seeing the gorgeous animal again. Renya had never been obsessed with horses, unlike other girls growing up, but after looking into the animal's intelligent eyes, she had to admit Starlia was special. She patted the mare carefully on the nose while Grayden tied a couple of sleeping rolls to the mare's back and filled the saddlebags with the supplies Eileen and Sari procured.

Grayden came up behind Renya and held out a lotus apple. She smiled and took it and held it out in front of the large animal's nose. Starlia opened her mouth and grabbed the apple from her palm.

Renya gasped. "Her tongue is purple!"

Grayden laughed. "That's the way of horses here. What color are their tongues in your land?"

Renya thought. "I actually don't know," she admitted, laughing. "Maybe pink? But definitely not purple."

She gave Starlia another pat and then waited for Grayden to help her up. If Starlia was just a bit shorter she might be able to climb up herself, but the animal was just too large. Grayden grasped her by the waist and made sure she was steady in the saddle before joining behind her. Renya arranged her full skirts around her, wishing she could have put on the leggings she had worn on her first ride. She fidgeted with the dress a little more before finally giving up.

"You don't wear dresses in your land?" Grayden asked, urging Starlia to trot.

"No, not every day at least, and not long and full-skirted like this. I mostly wore jeans and sweatshirts. Shorts and tank tops when I was in California."

Grayden looked at her thoughtfully. "It'll take us at least a full day, maybe more, to get back to Snowden Lodge. Why don't you tell me a little about your world?"

"Well, it's warmer than this..."

"Is that why you were so exposed when I found you?"

Renya laughed. "Compared to the beaches in California, I was way overdressed."

Grayden looked at her in disbelief.

"Most women wear bikinis at the beach. They just cover..." she blushed, not sure she wanted to continue.

"The parts that are different between a man and a woman?" Grayden asked, grinning as if he enjoyed her shyness.

"Well...yes..." Renya said, a bit flustered.

"If we get a portal opened, you'll have to take me to this California place."

Renya blushed a deep scarlet, which she guessed was Grayden's goal. He changed the subject and she appreciated him sparing her from further embarrassment.

"Tell me about your childhood," he implored.

"There's not much to tell. Like I said, my aunt raised me after my parents died. No siblings. My aunt never married, so it was just me and her. She taught me a lot. She wanted me to be strong, you know? And independent. That's probably why I studied so hard in school."

"What level of schooling did you get through?" Grayden asked.

"I finished up my university studies."

Grayden looked impressed. "What did you study there?"

"Communications," Renya replied.

"Ah! So you can speak many languages? Tell me, just human languages or the languages of many worlds?"

Renya suppressed a laugh. "No, Communications is how to deliver news to different audiences."

"So...you studied to be a messenger?" he asked.

"Kinda, if you stop interrupting, I could actually tell you."

"My apologies, dear Renya. Tell me all about communications."

"Well, you learn how to write well. And before you ask, no, not how to actually write. Human kids all learn that. You learn how to convey information, how to reach people. I specialized in journalism. Before I...I used to write for a newspaper. Do you have anything like that here?"

"We do." Grayden said. "We have bound papers delivered all around the kingdom. So you write those?"

"Yes, in a way. I wrote articles specifically around politics."

"I admire a woman interested in politics. Did you enjoy writing these articles?"

"I used to..." Renya began, but faltered.

"It's a long ride," Grayden reminded her, as Starlia galloped along a worn trail. In some spots, it was so bare she could see the soil underneath.

"I did like it. In fact, I loved it. I still do. But, I got involved with a married politician. He said he would help me with my career. I was naïve and believed him."

Grayden's powerful jaw clenched, and she felt his muscular arms tighten around her.

"He tried...he attacked me," Renya whispered, her voice barely audible over Starlia's hoofbeats.

Grayden looked like his blood was going to boil. His face was crimson and Renya noticed a throbbing vein in his neck. She had forgotten just how large and powerful he was. This man was fearsome. No matter how comfortable Renya got with him or how gentle he seemed, she needed to remember he was a powerhouse. His entire body seemed to tense, and she thought he stopped breathing altogether. She touched his arm, trying to get him to relax. He looked down at her hand on his forearm, and let out a few ragged breaths.

"You wanna know the worst part, Grayden? The media saw me leave his office...looking disheveled like I did...and they thought I was having an affair with him."

"Renya," Grayden said, his voice coming out strangled. "I'm so sorry. It seems to me your world doesn't treat women fairly."

She sighed. Her world didn't. Was his world any better? Time would tell. "So I did the only thing I thought I could. I ran away. I moved a thousand miles away and tried to forget it. Now I'm an entire world away...but the pain is still there."

Grayden didn't respond, but he pulled Renya closer to his chest. She let herself relax into his embrace, enjoying the sensation of closeness with another person. It had been a long time since she was held like this. In fact, she wasn't sure if she had ever been held like this. She felt safe and protected. Despite the strange situation she found herself in, she felt that perhaps she could trust this man.

Neither one said anything for a long while as they sought comfort in each other's arms.

Chapter Sixteen

G rayden took deep breaths as he tried to calm himself while Renya told her story. How dare someone touch her! And against her will. It sickened him. Grayden was going to open a portal and find the man and...no. He would not do that. He couldn't do that. His magic was weak. But that didn't mean *he* was. As his powers faded, he improved himself in other ways. He trained with Phillippe, read, met with advisors, studied, learned the land...he never wanted to worry about relying on magic. But then Queen Cressida made it a necessity again. He hoped Renya might help. He felt she was brought here for a reason and he longed to uncover it, along with the mystery of why he seemed to be inexplicably drawn to her.

They hadn't spoken for a long while. She was no longer holding herself away from him and instead, let herself relax in his arms. He enjoyed the closeness. Apart from a hug from Selenia or a pat on the back from Phillippe, he hadn't been touched by anyone for a long while, let alone embraced. He loved how peaceful she was in his arms. He thought she was asleep for a moment, but she was looking straight ahead at the trail. Grayden could see bare earth below the snow. Another sign of the Snow Land's weakening.

"Tell me about how you got here," Grayden prompted. He wanted more information about her, about how she might fit into their kingdom. But he was also curious to learn more about her.

"Curiosity. And books. A fondness for books," she replied. "There was a bookstore across the street from my apartment—an apartment is like a very tiny house—and I noticed people kept going in but not leaving. I went to check it out and there was a large hallway full of doors, but this one door, it just, kind of called to me. It was like I absolutely needed something on the other side of the door, or it needed me maybe, and the next thing I knew, I was here."

Grayden looked thoughtful. "I'm guessing you were in a Portal Corridor. It's a spot where lots of portals come together and people can travel easily from one spot to another. I hadn't heard of one connected to our lands for quite some time."

"Well, whatever it was, it brought me here."

"I'm glad it did," Grayden said. "You are awfully entertaining."

Renya playfully hit him, and Grayden laughed. "See, I don't think I've laughed this much in years. And in the face of battles and dragons and—"

"Dragons?" Renya groaned. "Please don't tell me they are real!"

"Very real, I'm afraid. That's what got to my men at the border. There was a long battle, but it quickly concluded when the dragons arrived. It doesn't bode well for the future of this world. The dragons were brought through a portal, even bigger and more powerful than the one you went through. The Shadow Queen's power continues to grow."

Renya moved in closer to Grayden's chest. "Do they breathe fire?"

"Fire?" Grayden asked. "No, they don't breathe fire. But they are intelligent and brutal. They can also call upon elements. I'm guessing that is where your fire breathing fable might come from. They can shift the atmosphere and the climate. You can see along the path here, the closer south we are, the snowdrifts are more shallow and in some spots you can see bare earth. I had thought it was the magic fading or the influence of the Shadow Queen's power, but now I wonder if it's the work of the dragons."

"So your brother leads the armies? And patrols the borders?"

"Yes, it's what he prefers. We both have an equal say in how things are done," he explained. "While Phillippe is the eldest and therefore entitled to our father's crown, he possesses no power. He was born without magic. As the first born magical child, the line of succession goes to me."

"So...you're a king?"

"Does that impress you, Little Fawn?" Grayden teased. He had a feeling that Renya didn't put much stock into birthrights. "All but in name, I guess you could say. Some still call me prince, others lord. It didn't feel honorable taking what should have been my brother's. Phillippe is incredibly skilled in other things and does well without magic. There's no reason he shouldn't lead. But he prefers to look out for our borders and generally leaves political matters to me. But we both play a crucial role in ensuring the survival of the Snow Lands."

"So it's just you and your brother?" Renya asked.

"A sister too. Younger than you, I think. She'll be nineteen next month. Selenia."

"Pretty name," Renya commented.

"Yes, but not as beautiful as Renya. Do you know your name is an old Fae name?"

Renya stared at him. "No, I had no idea. I don't even know my middle name. My aunt could never find my birth certificate. Aunt Agatha said my parents must have had a home birth. She ended up getting a delayed birth certificate shortly after she took me in."

Grayden chewed his bottom lip. He wondered if he should tell her now what he suspected. Every time she talked about her past, he seemed more and more certain she might have Fae heritage. He didn't want to upset her without being certain, so he held his tongue. But he wanted to give her something, at least. "Renya means 'bringer of light'," he said quietly.

She looked at him critically. "Really? Why would I have a Fae name?"

"It's not terribly uncommon. As travel increased between our worlds, Fae culture became blended with human culture and I'm sure the opposite has occurred. Look at your knowledge of dragons. They don't exist in your world, but somehow bits of knowledge about them passed through the portals."

Renya looked placated by the answer. "So tell me about Selenia," she asked, looking out into the distance. They had covered quite a bit of ground, and Grayden tried to view his lands as Renya must. The Snow lands were a vast, wintery expanse for those unfamiliar with them. He, however, could tell sudden changes in the lands, curves and dense forests that helped guide him.

A sweet smile crossed Grayden's face. He adored his sister. "She's mischievous and a bit stubborn. She reminds me of you, in that sense," he said, nudging her a bit with his shoulder. "But she's caring and sweet, too.

She loves animals of all kinds. And music. She has a good ear and likes to sing. It took her a year after our parents died to sing again, though. I imagine it was the hardest on her. No mother to help guide her. Especially now she's approaching marriageable age. I don't know how to handle it. I dread her coming of age almost as much as I dread what's happening to our land."

"Spoken like a protective older brother," Renya said, winking.

"Of that, I am guilty. She's been getting closer to her guard, Jurel. She can be a bit too used to getting her way, and she has charm as well as beauty. If she sets her sights on him, I'm afraid putting her off will be difficult for him."

"Is it an unsuitable match?" Renya asked. "Is she limited on who she can marry?"

"It could be considered so by some. There are those who would expect her to marry a royal from another realm. It's not just about royalty marrying royalty, but trying to have the best odds of producing magical heirs. The royal lines tend to be the purest and have the most magical blood."

"I see." Renya pursed her lips.

"You think it's wrong?" guessed Grayden.

"It's not that I think it's wrong, it's just sad that is what is expected of your sister."

"You misunderstand me, Renya. I wish Selenia to marry for love. I've denied requests for her hand from many noble families."

He knew he had shocked her, and hoped the rough edges of her armor were slowly loosening. He wanted her to trust him, to believe he had her best interests at heart, even though he wasn't sure why it should matter to him.

"And what about Prince Grayden?" she mocked. "Will he marry for love?"

He was silent for a long moment. "I'm not free to marry."

Grayden sensed the tension going through her body. Something about what he said bothered her. But why should it? He clarified at any rate.

"There might be a time in the future where a marriage alliance could save my lands from destruction. I must keep myself free in case this...struggle...with our world can't be managed with anything else."

"What are you going to do about the Shadow Queen?" Renya asked softly, her body relaxing after his answer. He wondered for a split second if she was worried that he was already promised to someone.

"Whatever I must. Find more men, seek answers from some of our seers, infiltrate her court with spies... we have a man there, but he's gone silent. I worry his double role has been uncovered. I've also sent word to some of the other realms. Mainly, the Tidal Kingdom and the Twilight Kingdom. They liked my father and allied with him previously. I'm hoping we can work together now to halt the threat. Maybe they have knowledge I don't or their powers might be stronger."

"It sounds like you are doing everything you can."

"Almost everything," he sighed. "The Shadow Queen wants to unite our kingdoms through marriage."

"You mean she wants to marry into your family?"

"Yes. As the eldest, it should be Phillippe. But he has no magic, so she wouldn't get magical heirs, which is what she's really after. She wants a prodigy with power." He exhaled loudly.

"So she wants you."

He paused for a long while, trying to decide how much he wanted to tell her. Finally he answered. "Yes. She seeks a marriage alliance with me. I've refused her. And it's not just because she's older than me by half, or that I don't love her. If I thought it was the right thing for my people, I would do it in a heartbeat, even if I lived in misery for the rest of my life. I'm worried it's the wrong move for our people. I believe she'll use me as a stepping stone to get to my armies and my lands."

"I'm sorry, Grayden," Renya said.

"Me too," he replied, squeezing her a bit tighter. Neither said anything for the next hour. The sun was starting to set, and Grayden slowly halted Starlia as they came across a large snowbank. It formed a u-shape around them. There was also a small stream nearby, mostly frozen, but with some water trickling through under the ice.

"I think this is a good place to stop for the night," Grayden announced. "The sun is setting earlier and earlier and I don't want to be traveling in the dark with so many unknowns. I'll start a fire and get the tent set up, but let's get a some water first. Can you take this water pouch and go fill it up at the stream?"

He watched as Renya took the leather bag and sludged through the crystal snow to the little stream. Clear ice covered the top, but underneath he knew there would be water racing down, following a path away from the snowbank and down a little hill. The trees in the area were bare, and the leafless edges looked harsh and jagged compared to the cool blanket of snow covering the hillside.

He started to put up the tent, but couldn't take his eyes off of her by the stream. Kneeling, Renya pushed her skirts aside and used the dried wood to poke a hole in the ice and fill up the pouch. When the cold water dribbled outside of the top, Renya stood up to head back to where Grayden was setting up the tent. He quickly shifted his eyes away, not wanting to be seen watching her so closely.

"Grayden!" she called out, in a hoarse whisper.

Panicking, Grayden joined her side just as the graceful animal lowered her head down to the frozen water.

"What is it?" she asked, trying not to move her lips.

"It's an elkten," Grayden said. "It's actually my animal guardian." He lowered himself a bit, trying to minimize his large form.

"What?" Renya asked, still staring at the animal. They watched as the elkten took her star-shaped hoof and pressed it down until she cracked the ice. She gently pressed her lips against the hole she'd made and drank at the trickling water.

"When children are born in our realm, a master seer peers into what they call 'the fire of knowledge' and interprets what the babe's guide will be. The guide is said to appear to them at significant times in the person's life and signal life changes or important events are about to pass."

Renya gasped as two baby elkten pranced out happily from behind the snowbank. They approached their mother, hiding slightly behind her legs, as they joined her in drinking.

"They are gray while she's white," she mused.

"I think they turn white as they get older." Grayden's voice was hardly above a whisper. "We've thought them all but extinct. I can't believe I've seen them not once, but twice along this journey. And twin fawns as well! Tumwalt will have to eat his words. I'd heard the rumors, but he dismissed them."

"Who is Tumwalt?" she asked, not taking her eyes off the babies.

"He's my most trusted advisor," he said. "Tumwalt served my father and now he serves me. He means well, he just doesn't understand that I'm not my father."

They watched the fawns and their mother for a little longer. The twin fawns continued to drink from the opening their mother had made and then frolicked in the snow. One baby found a small stick and dragged it over to where the mother stood. She nipped at the stick, sniffing it, and then quickly lost interest. The mother started walking away from the stream, her babies following behind, until they disappeared back behind the snow drift. Renya let out a loud exhale, and Grayden did as well. He didn't realize he'd been holding his breath until they disappeared.

Grayden rose from his crouched position with ease, his strong thigh muscles lifting him up quickly. "Come along Renya, it's getting dark."

He took her gloved hand and guided her back to where he had set up the tent and started a fire. She untied their sleeping rolls from Starlia, and Grayden lightened her saddle bags. Free from the extra weight, she whinnied and galloped away without looking back.

"Where's she going?" Renya asked, her tone anxious.

"Don't be alarmed, our mode of transportation isn't running away," he teased. "She's just going to graze. It's also near the end of her season, so she might be trying to find a handsome stallion to mount her." He winked at Renya, and watched the redness appear in her cheeks. He didn't know why, but he loved when her neck and cheeks turned that slight pink shade. Anytime she blushed, he felt excitement in a way he knew he shouldn't.

Grayden dragged over a large fallen tree trunk for them to sit on. He moved it easily, placing it before the fire and sitting on it. He brushed it free of snow and then motioned for Renya to come sit beside him. Grayden took out a couple of wrapped parcels from one of the bags Starlia had been carrying and handed one to Renya. She took off her gloves and opened it, finding a sweet candied cake with some type of dried nut on top of it, some cheese and dried meat.

Grayden pulled out a small pot and began adding some herbs, dried fruits, and a handful of snow before setting it to rest in the fire. The flames licked their way up the sides of the pot while the snow melted. Soon, a familiar citrus smell warmed the air.

"Is that the drink you tried to give me when I first woke up?" Renya asked.

"You have a sharp nose," he replied. "Yes, it's crimling tea. It has bark from the crimling tree to sweeten it, and different dried citrus fruits in it. It can also calm you and help you sleep."

"Where did you learn to make it?"

"When I was fifteen, my father sent me off to train with one of his troops. It was further north, deep in the mountains, and even colder than it is here. The soldiers make and drink a lot of hot beverages."

"I'm glad I'll get to taste it this time. I was so weak when you found me, I think I passed out right before I could," Renya said.

Grayden wondered if he should tell her what transpired with her mark and that his healer thought she was touched by Fae magic. Did she even know she had the mark? He hesitated, not sure whether it was better to be honest with her now, when he wasn't sure and didn't have the answers he knew she'd need, or if he should wait until they saw Almory. He decided honesty was the best in the situation, and they would hopefully be back at the lodge soon and Almory might have the answers she needed. "Renya, I need to tell—"

She spoke at the same time. "I haven't really said it, but thank you for helping me that night, and I guess last night and this night, too. I—I have trouble trusting people, well, men in particular, but I'm so grateful it was you who found me. You seem like a decent man."

Grayden opened his mouth to tell her about his suspicions about her origins, but at that moment she put her petite hand on top of his thigh, just above the knee. Instantly, Grayden's stomach clenched and a wave of heat rushed to his groin. He shifted uncomfortably as he felt his body come to life. He didn't want to scare her or make her think he expected anything out of her in return for assisting her, but her touch awoke a hunger in him that he hadn't experienced in quite some time.

While he pondered his response, Renya quickly removed her hand.

Grayden cleared his throat, trying to repair the damage he had done by not responding fast enough. "Renya, I'm sorry, it's just that—"

"Please, don't say anything more. I don't know what I was thinking. I just...I don't know. Can we forget it?"

Grayden looked into her ceruleum blue eyes and then down at her full lips. He didn't want to forget it. He wanted...something he shouldn't want. Something he shouldn't ask for or hope for when he promised to help her leave his world. Afraid his voice would be full of lust and betray him, he simply nodded, his mess of dark hair falling into his eyes.

"Thank you. I'm going to go in the tent and try to get warm." Renya stood up and quickly headed into the tent.

Grayden sat on the log and looked into the fire for a long time, unseeing. What was he doing? He couldn't let this woman get close to him. She was going to go home. Plus, this senator person had taken advantage of her. He didn't know exactly what a senator was, but he imagined it was a person in a position of power. Someone who should have looked after her virtue, not taken it. Grayden tried to push down the images of Renya, trembling and scared, while a man forced himself into her. Instantly, his whole body was hot, and it had nothing to do with the crackling flames in front of him. His muscles raged, full of fury. He wanted to annihilate this man who dared to touch his woman. He was going to—no. She wasn't his woman. Fates, he needed to find out who exactly she was and then get her through a portal and back to her own world. His honor was hanging by a thread where Renya was concerned, and he was afraid every hour spent in her presence was slowly plucking away at the thin string.

Chapter Seventeen

Renya woke up in the small tent just as the sun was rising. She felt oddly warm in the sleeping roll. It was lined with some type of waterproof skin and the thick, wooly fur on top held in all of her body heat. Her nose and ears were the only part of her body feeling cold. She looked over to where she had set out Grayden's sleeping roll the night before, only to find it missing. Where was he? He didn't sleep outside all night, did he? She pushed herself out of the warm furs with a groan and crawled toward the flap of the tent. A fresh layer of snow covered the log. Starlia had returned, and was drinking from the stream. She saw another snow covered log next to the fire, and then realized it was Grayden. She marched over to him, furious.

"What are you doing out here?" she yelled, eyes flaring with anger at his stupidity. "You could have frozen to death, you damn idiot!" She had no idea why she was so mad, but her blood was boiling at the thought of him endangering himself unnecessarily.

Grayden rolled over onto his back and stared up at her. "It wasn't proper for me to share the tent with you, Renya. And of course, I would not let you sleep outside."

Renya fumed. "And it's proper for you to nearly freeze to death? You could get frostbite, or hypothermia, or—"

Grayden stretched his arms as she continued her

tirade, a small grin on his face.

"Are you even listening to me?" she accused.

"I'm sure you are making excellent points, dear Renya. But I'm afraid that those points, along with the whole reason I slept outside, are almost moot at the moment."

"Why?" she asked irritatedly, crossing her arms in front of her.

"You're standing over me and with the way the wind is blowing…I can see up your skirts."

If he thought she was angry before, it was nothing compared to now. She went to storm away, but she felt him tug on her arm and pull her warm body into his cold one.

"Don't worry, Little Fawn," he said, slowly running his freezing hands up and back down her sides. He leaned in and whispered in her ear. "I won't tell anyone."

She shoved him away and started packing up their campsite.

He laughed, seeming to enjoy their little argument.

Once everything from their makeshift camp was packed up, Grayden lifted Renya onto Starlia, and she cried out suddenly.

"What's wrong?" he asked, instantly alarmed.

"Nothing. I'm just…sore," she confessed. The long ride took its toll on her body, although she hated to admit it to him.

"I think we should be back to the lodge by mid-day," he said. "In the meantime, if it would make it easier on you, you could ride side-saddle."

Renya was torn. While riding side-saddle would ease the ache she felt along her thighs, she'd lose stability and have to rely on Grayden more. Ever since he flinched when she had placed her hand on his thigh, she felt uncertain about any physical contact they made.

Starlia fidgeted a bit. The animal started moving around, eager to go, and the slight movement sent a pain through Renya's back and she conceded.

"Okay, I think that's my only option at this point," she said, and swung her leg back over and balanced herself.

Grayden looked pleased at himself for winning an argument with her for once, and she swallowed her annoyance at him besting her. She felt him gather her closer in his arms and set Starlia at a bit of a slower speed. Renya could tell the animal was irritated at the restraint and wanted to run, but she was grateful for the slower pace Grayden's set.

"Something funny there, popsicle boy?" Renya asked. Now that she was riding side-saddle, she could see his facial expressions fully. He had a boyish grin on his face, and he looked so young with his wild hair mussed from sleeping outside.

"Popsicle? What in the Gods' names is that?"

Renya chortled. "It's what stupid men turn into when they sleep outside all night in freezing temperatures." She pushed her hair out of her face as Starlia continued to sprint across the unforgiving landscape.

"Fine. I promise never to sleep outside again. Are you happy?"

She suppressed a giggle. Actually, she was happy. Renya felt free in a way she'd never felt before. There was no pressure, no rent to worry about, no dread when she got a google alert that the senator was mentioned somewhere, and, of course, her name tied in.

"Well, I'm at least happy you've decided not to be a moron."

"I'll take that as a yes." Again, that schoolboy grin. One side of his lip curled higher than the other when he smiled, and he had the tiniest hint of a dimple on his left cheek. He was quite charming, Renya admitted to herself. His arm muscles flexed with every slight adjustment he made on the reins, and Renya tried not to stare.

They continued their journey and Renya's stomach growled and she was thinking of asking Grayden to stop for a break. Suddenly, Starlia reared back, whining. Her eyes were darting frantically, searching the surrounding woods, her sharp nose sniffing the air. Grayden barely caught Renya in time as the mare reared again, nearly throwing them both off her back.

"Stay quiet!" Grayden commanded, pulling the sword he carried off of his back. His movements were swift and sure. It was obvious to Renya that he was a skilled warrior.

"What's going on—"

Renya froze as she saw a dozen pairs of eyes emerge from up ahead. Growling and practically vibrating with agitation, she counted at least twelve strange beasts stalking towards them. They had yellow eyes that seemed to glow even in the daylight. Their snouts looked wolfish but the animals had great red manes running down their thick neck. Their bodies were gray and speckled with black. The tail was impressive, almost the entire span of its body, and came to a point with a large, sharp spike. The biggest animal was in front, with the others behind it in a v-like formation.

"Tygres," Grayden said, and tried to turn Starlia

in the other direction, but she wouldn't budge. The poor horse was afraid, paralyzed with fear. "Renya, swing your leg back around. I'm going to need both hands. Hold on tight to the pommel of the saddle."

The front tygre leapt so fast, it looked like a blur. Starlia reared up again, but quickly took off for the clearing. Renya could hear the howls of the animals behind them, and fear lurched in her stomach. The leader of the pack jumped up with his vicious teeth bared, and Renya could feel his hot breath as he tried to lunge at her, jaws snapping. Before she could react, Grayden's sword pierced through the animal's mouth and back through the other side. Renya didn't even have time to process as the animal fell on to the soft snow.

Another tygre came from the other side, and Starlia swerved to dodge it. The unexpected directional change threw Grayden to the side and off of the horse's back.

"No!" Renya screamed in terror. She grabbed Starlia's reins and tried to force the animal back towards Grayden, who was lying on his back with a sword in one hand and a small dagger in the other. Starlia let out a huge whine and tried to make for the woods on the other side of the clearing.

Renya looked over her shoulder as two of the beasts lunged at Grayden. He pushed them off of him and made quick work of both. However, a third tygre was circling and took the opportunity to attack from the side. He slashed Grayden across the chest, and Renya could see the blood splatter on the snow. Her stomach turned, nauseated at the sight of his crimson blood against the pure, white snow. With a swift flash of Grayden's dagger, the animal was down.

She continued to try to urge Starlia back towards Grayden, but it was hopeless. The stubborn horse pranced and trotted just outside of the thick forest, avoiding the carnage. Renya dismounted and fell into a large snowdrift. She rushed toward Grayden, her feet sinking in the deep snow. It was like a nightmare where she was being chased but couldn't run, her feet stuck and unmoving.

"Stay back!" Grayden shouted at Renya. Another animal rushed at him and with a swing of his sword, the animal went down quickly.

"No!" Renya screamed, as another one of the beasts tried to attack Grayden. His sword and dagger were knocked out of reach.

Renya finally reached him, picked up the fallen dagger and lodged it in the tygre's back with a groan of exertion. The animal fell, and Grayden rolled him off.

She looked at the dagger in the animal's back and watched Grayden pull it out and wipe it clean on the animal's fur. Renya felt sick again as she saw its sticky blood run out onto the snow. She couldn't believe she had done that. Renya hadn't even thought about it, she just acted.

The rest of the animals drew back, sensing the loss of half of their pack. They howled as they headed back toward the forest. The sound sent a shiver down Renya's spine.

She quickly knelt at Grayden's side. He was losing a lot of blood from the wound on his chest.

"That was...not a risk...I would have you take, Renya," Grayden said, wincing in pain, his breath ragged. "You should have stayed on Starlia and fled."

"Would you just shut up for a second while I decide

what to do with your wound?" Renya glanced at Starlia, who had trotted back over now the danger had passed. "Are there any kind of medical supplies in the packs?"

"Yes, there should be a parcel from Dimitri," Grayden said, attempting to sit back up.

"Don't you dare sit up," Renya scolded as she approached the mare and tore apart the bags before she found what she was looking for. "I need to clean the wound. It's dirty, and those animals left...foamy, sticky saliva in it."

"Lovely," grunted Grayden. "What a nice parting gift to leave me with...fireale will do the trick to clean it out, it's in the second saddle bag."

Renya found the bottle of the reddish liquid and then tore Grayden's shirt the rest of the way so she could work. She poured the liquid over the wound to flush it and Grayden grimaced a bit, but didn't flinch. She went through the bag and found a needle and thread. Renya poured some more fireale out on her hands to disinfect them.

"Hey, leave some fireale for me."

Renya ignored him, but then thought it might not be a bad idea for him to be relaxed. She needed him to be still if she was going to attempt this. She pressed the bottle to his lips, and he drank deep.

"Are you ready?" she questioned, needle threaded, but hands shaking.

"Do I have a choice?"

"No," she said, as she inserted the first stitch. He groaned a bit, and took another drink of the fireale, cradling the bottle in his arms.

Soon, the fireale was gone, and Renya was tying off the thread. After the first few stitches, she stopped shaking and focused on what she was doing. She couldn't believe she'd stitched him up. As a girl, she had fallen off her bicycle and gashed her knee along the chain link fence in the neighbor's yard. She had watched the doctor stitch up her leg, fascinated. At this moment, she was incredibly grateful for her natural curiosity and how observant she was.

Renya looked at her patient and saw there was no way he was fit to travel. He was practically slobbering drunk. She sighed and decided they needed to wait it out. She didn't even think he could sit upright on Starlia. His face was relaxed and his shoulders loose. She hadn't seen him so peaceful since she'd met him. She didn't know how it was possible, but he looked even more striking with his calm features and the stressed look he often wore completely gone.

Determined, Renya got to work setting up camp. Grayden had said they only had a couple of hours of travel left, but she didn't think it was wise to travel after dark, especially with Grayden so inebriated. If she let Grayden sleep it off overnight, they should still reach his lodge well before noon the next day.

She set up the tent and started a fire. Grayden tried to help, but he was more of a hindrance in his current state. Satisfied with the fire she had started, she helped Grayden sit in front of it before settling herself near him, looking after her patient.

"Why does it get so dark so early here?" she asked him.

"The magic," he said thickly, tripping over his words. "It's...out of balance. It needs to be balanced. I have to fix it. I'll probably have to marry that evil witch at some point."

"The Shadow Queen?"

"Yup, that's the one," he sighed. "Either that or marry Selenia to an asshole. But I can't do that. But Renya, the Shadow Queen...she's so...old." He fumbled around with the words, and Renya tried not to laugh at him. He said the word 'old' like it was the worst possible thing a person could be. "And every second I don't marry her, she gets even older."

"If she's so old, can she even produce an heir?" Renya asked.

"Unfortunately, yes. But...oh Fates. The thought of merely kissing her makes my stomach sick. I couldn't—I mean, how could anyone—?"

"Grayden, maybe you should go to the tent and sleep before you get sick. You've had too much to drink."

"No, I'm guarding you."

Renya didn't have the heart to tell him he was barely sitting upright and, rather, she was watching him.

"Oh, pretty Renya," he sighed, leaning towards her. "Why can't you be the Shadow Queen? You're young and spirited. You would be so much better for me. We'd have fun together, I know it."

This time, she laughed. "I'm also not a homicidal maniac, so there's that, too."

"Yeah, that's true as well." He leaned against her and Renya could smell the fireale on his breath. Her pulse quickened at the contact.

"How does your chest feel?" she asked him, concerned about his wound.

"Tight," he replied. "Like someone is squeezing it. But that's just because you're sitting near me." He looked up at her adoringly.

"Whoa there, lover boy. I think it's time for you to

get some rest. Why don't you go lay out the sleeping rolls in the tent?"

"That's a good idea. You're so smart Renya. And you're pretty too." He leaned down and managed to place a chaste kiss on her forehead before heading toward the tent, stumbling a bit. He tripped, knees sinking into the snow, but then managed to get up and finally disappeared into the tent.

Renya felt bad for laughing at him. But he was hilariously drunk. She sat near the fire, thinking about everything that happened today. He said being near him was dangerous, and boy, he was right. But she also felt proud of herself, too. Powerful. She wondered if this is what Aunt Agatha had been training her for, all those nights in the woods learning how to live off the land. Did she know? Had she thought this might happen to her? She couldn't help but think about her aunt's warning about the bookstore. Did she know about portals? Renya wasn't even sure she'd ever get to see her again to ask her. She sighed and decided she better go check on Grayden.

She made her way over to the tent and looked inside. Grayden was curled up on top of his sleeping roll, passed out. His boots were still on and his sword was wrapped over his shoulder. Renya reached over and gently untangled it from his arms and set it next to him. Renya watched his chest rise and fall and then crawled further into the tent. He had left quite the trail of blood in the snow, and she was worried he might have lost too much.

She spread out the sleeping roll next to him and snuggled down inside. Renya watched him while he breathed in and then back out again. She studied his face. He was scruffier than when she first met him, but his sharp jawline was still easily distinguishable. His features were entirely masculine, but his eyes, which were currently closed, softened him. His unruly hair crept forward over his forehead, and Renya pushed it back out of his face. It was surprisingly soft under her fingertips. She played with a lock between her fingers. She wondered just how old he was. When he was awake, commanding his armies and protecting her, he seemed far older than her. But here on the furs, his forehead unfurrowed and his lips full and slightly parted, he looked so young. Much younger than she would have guessed. Too young to have such a heavy burden placed on him. She watched him breathe for just a few more minutes, trying to convince herself she just wanted to make sure he was okay. But the minutes ticked by and she couldn't pull her eyes away from his handsome profile.

Chapter Eighteen

G rayden woke up with a splitting headache. Fates, what had happened? He remembered drink...and more drink...He rubbed his eyelids and winced at the movement. Ah yes...he was injured. And Renya stitched him up, she–

He sat up quickly, looking for her. His eyes landed on her sleeping frame next to him. Not just next to him. She was pressed warmly to his side, her blonde hair falling over her shoulders and tumbling down his bare chest. She sighed in her sleep, her little lips pressed together. Grayden couldn't take his eyes off of her and lay there, mesmerized by her. She was a beautiful woman, he admitted to himself. Waking up beside her in this tent was far better than sleeping outside like he had the night before. For a second, maybe a minute, he could pretend that his life was different, and he was free to do what he wished. He imagined waking up in the morning next to a wife he loved, eager to spend the day with her and making love at night.

She was one of the first women he'd ever met who had no issue putting him in his place. He loved when she argued with him, full of fire and spirit. He thought back to the morning before when she yelled at him for sleeping outside. She looked beautiful, with snowflakes in her tangled hair and her eyes wide. He had resisted the urge to pull her to him and kiss her until her mouth stilled and quieted underneath his.

It had been a rough few days for her, and he honestly couldn't believe the strength she possessed. She handled the situation remarkably well, and he admired her. Not only was she beautiful, but she was intelligent and accomplished. He hoped Selenia grew up to be strong like her. Grayden wondered what Selenia would make of Renya. He could see them now, whispering and conspiring against him. It brought a smile to his lips and, for the first time in a while, he let himself imagine a future that didn't end with a miserable and strategic marriage to a stranger.

Knowing they had to get moving, but still hating himself for it, he stroked her arm to wake her. She moaned in her sleep, and the sound was so primal that Grayden inwardly groaned with arousal.

Renya slowly awoke and turned towards Grayden. She realized how close she was to him and pushed herself off of the furs. She must have sought out his body heat after she fell asleep, not realizing how close she was, but he didn't mind.

"How are you feeling?" she asked.

"Can you ask me that question tomorrow?" He squinted his eyes at the light in the tent.

"I can't say I'm surprised," Renya said, inspecting the cloth bound around his chest where she had stitched him up. Grayden glanced down, and was relieved to see minimal blood on it, and felt proud of the job Renya had done. "You seemed determined to finish the whole bottle off."

Grayden groaned, looking at her. "I hardly remember anything," he said sheepishly.

"You should be glad," she replied, eyes sparkling

mischievously. "You took all your clothing off and ran around the forest naked."

He paled. She giggled, and he smiled at her. "You basically just passed out after accusing the Shadow Queen of being really old," she laughed. A warmth passed between them, and Grayden was suddenly very aware of the fact she was next to him, in a tent, with nothing but the quiet wind outside. Her lips parted involuntarily, and her eyes widened. He leaned towards her and gently twirled a lock of her golden hair around his fingers. He watched the way it changed color in the light. Emerald eyes met sky blue ones. Grayden reached out tentatively and tucked the lock of hair behind her ear as Renya took a shaky breath. He raised his hand cautiously to touch her cheek.

Before he could make contact, Starlia whined, jolting their attention. Suddenly, the tent seemed too small and Renya rushed out. Grayden followed behind, coldness hitting his body and cooling his blood. They silently gathered up the supplies once more, and Starlia stood impatiently as they loaded her down. Grayden managed to get himself up into the saddle, but they had to find a fallen log for Renya to step on and mount the mare. Renya said didn't want to take any chances of his stitches ripping, even though Grayden protested strongly.

Starlia's hooves pounded against the snow as they continued out of the clearing and into another forest. Grayden watched Renya stare at the horizon, keeping her eyes peeled for danger.

"What exactly were those animals?" she asked Grayden.

"Tygres," he replied. "I've never seen them this far north before. They belong in the Shadow Realm. I'm guessing this was just another attack orchestrated by Queen Cressida. She hopes to weaken us and force my hand..." he stopped short of what he was going to say.

"Force you to do what?" Renya asked, turning her neck to look back at him.

"Reconsider the marriage alliance."

"Oh. You seemed pretty against it last night."

"I won't do it," Grayden said, adjusting the reins in his hands. "She'll only use my lands and take what little magic I have left. It's not an option I will ever consider."

He said it with such finality that he actually believed it himself, despite the desperation he felt to save his kingdom.

Renya looked forward, no doubt noticing a small village in the distance. "Grayden!" she exclaimed excitedly. "Look! Is that your home?"

"It is, and the whole town of Wesalie. The Snowden Lodge is past the town."

Renya began chatting animatedly. "I love Starlia, but I can't wait to be on solid ground. Do you have running water? Maybe I can take a bath?

He laughed again. "We do having running water. A hot bath would definitely help ease your aches and pains."

They approached the town, and Grayden watched Renya's eyes widen as she took in the first actual view of civilization in this land. The houses on the outskirts of the town were cute little farming cottages, with animals in covered stalls or grazing in white-covered meadows. As they got closer to the heart of the town, the gravel path beneath Starlia's hooves turned into neat little cobblestones, shoveled free of snow. The townhomes were small and stacked tidy, and shops of every nature appeared in between the homes. There was an old-fashioned smithy and a tannery, but also shops selling charms and amulets. A florist stood outside the shops, arranging a bouquet expertly. The stems were blue and the petals were the palest white. Yet the edges glistened under the sunlight. Grayden took note of her excitement, enjoying her pleasure in his home.

He knew the sights were beautiful, but it was nothing compared to the smell. There was a vendor selling roasted nuts, and the smell of cinnamon and pine from the surrounding forest made a unique scent that only existed here.

"What do you think, Little Fawn?"

"It's...breathtaking."

There were many people roaming the streets, shopping, talking, and laughing with bags in their hands. As Grayden passed by, low bows of the head followed in his wake until finally they passed the city in a blur. Up the hill, twinkling under ice and snow, was Snowden Lodge, and Grayden pointed it out to Renya proudly.

"Grayden, lodge is not the word I would use to describe it. I pictured a an old victorian-age hunting cabin."

A gray castle stretched in front of them with flags hanging from torrents, and smoke rising from chimneys all over. A simple gate warded off intruders, and as Starlia made her way up the familiar path, two men opened the gates and they arrived in a little courtyard. A few men came running out to steady Starlia, and Grayden gently slid off, holding his injured side cautiously. He motioned for one of the grooms to help Renya down, and the larger of the two men came forward and grabbed her waist, setting her down next to Grayden. He felt another flurry of desire along with a fury of anger when the groom helped her down. The second the groom released her, Grayden moved over and pulled her closer to him.

"My lord!" a voice called from a doorway off of the courtyard. Grayden smiled as the middle-aged man, hastened towards them and gave a low bow. He wore a tunic similar to the one Grayden wore, and a pearly polar bear crest rested against his chest.

"Tumwalt! Tell me, how is everything here?"

"About the same. Although Almory had a bit of luck translating more of the scroll and—"

"We can talk about it later. Let me first introduce you to Renya." Grayden gestured to Renya, and she stepped forward. Renya awkwardly nodded and dipped a bit.

Tumwalt's face crumpled briefly in confusion, and he brought his hand up to rub his bearded chin. But he smoothly hid it and gave Renya a bow as well. "Welcome to Snowden Lodge, Mistress Renya."

Renya offered him a shy smile.

"I think you have a lot to catch me up on," Tumwalt directed toward Grayden, his eyes glancing at Renya.

"That I do, Tumwalt," Grayden replied, gently slapping the man on the back. "But first, where is Doria? I'd like her to see to Renya. We've been traveling and I fear it hasn't been a peaceful journey."

"And Prince Phillippe?" Tumwalt inquired. "Your messenger arrived saying he was unconscious."

"He's awake now and seems to be doing better. It'll be awhile before he can travel, though. Although you know how he is, I'm sure Dimitri won't be able to deter him from getting home and back on the battlefield as soon as he can."

Out of the corner of her eye, Grayden caught a

woman bustling toward them.

"Ah! Doria!" Grayden said. "I'd like to introduce you to someone. This is Renya, and she is my personal guest. I would love it if you would make her feel welcome."

Doria bobbed her head and smiled warmly at Renya. If she found it odd that Prince Grayden had brought a girl back with him, she didn't show it. She simply grasped Renya's arm and strolled off in the entryway's direction. Renya gave a small smile back towards Grayden as she disappeared into his home.

Chapter Nineteen

T umwalt followed on Grayden's heels to his
bedchamber. He stood off to the side as Grayden
began removing his sword and dagger and putting on a
fresh tunic, trying to hide his injury the best he could.
Tumwalt didn't need the stress of having both brothers
injured, and he didn't want to make a fuss.

"What about the scrolls?" Grayden asked,
throwing his torn shirt on the bed. Tumwalt glanced at
the blood on the shirt but didn't comment. Grayden was
sure he assumed that it was Phillippe's blood, not his
own.

"Almory has deciphered at least half of it. A
few days ago, the guardian spell simply vanished. He's
very excited. He had to rework the original translation
through early elvenish, but he wants you to see him
straightaway."

"That's great," Grayden said. "It couldn't come at a
better time."

"My lord...can I ask about the girl?" Tumwalt
broached the subject carefully. Other than proposing
marriage alliances, Tumwalt mostly tried to stay out
of Grayden's romantic relationships, or rather, lack
of. Grayden was always quite discreet in his physical
relationships, and he was careful to never be seen publicly
with a woman.

Grayden tucked his tunic into a fresh pair of black

leather trousers and took a deep breath before starting. "I found her in the woods while we made camp. Tumwalt, she arrived from a portal."

Tumwalt's jaw dropped. "On our lands?"

"Yes. And not only that...Fae magic has marked her." Grayden lowered his voice, even though they were alone in his rooms. "She's an orphan and has no recollection of her parents. She's been raised by an aunt in the human world. But Tumwalt, I sense something about her... and she arrived after I saw an elkten in the woods along the borders."

Tumwalt's eyes widened. "And her name...Renya? That's an ancient Fae name...from the Spring Lands? Or maybe Sun?

"It's the Sun Realm." Grayden said with finality. "It means bringer of light."

Tumwalt looked absolutely astonished. "The scrolls...Almory said they mention the return of a light bringer."

Grayden felt he should be surprised, but he had such a strong feeling about Renya being important. At first, he thought he was merely attracted to her strength and beauty, but he knew deep down it was something more. He had sensed something in her. Was it her power? Whatever it was, it was muted, just underneath the surface. It was like hearing someone shout while your head was underwater. "I need to hear about this from Almory. And then I want him to meet Renya."

Tumwalt nodded, and they both hurried out the door and took the back staircases down to Almory's workshop.

Grayden pushed the heavy door open and the earthy smell of burning herbs greeted him. Almory was in the corner of the darkly lit space, writing on parchment with several enormous books opened all around him. He was muttering excitedly to himself and didn't even notice when they entered. It took almost a full minute before he looked up and saw his visitors.

"My prince! You've returned!" he squeaked. "I've made some amazing progress, I think you'll be quite pleased," he said, easing up from his chair and ambling toward the center of the room, where an ancient piece of parchment lay, protected under a glass dome. "Come, look!"

Grayden peered into the glass dome, seeing nothing but strange words and symbols moving around the parchment.

Almory took a pinch of a white powder and sprinkled it on the parchment. At once, the words slowed, and it was possible to make out the symbols, but Grayden couldn't read them. "You see!" Almory exclaimed proudly.

Grayden stared at him for a second. "Look, that's great Almory, but what does it say?"

Almory grabbed his glasses and read:

"When magic fades, light bringer returns,
Power will flow and lust will burn."

Grayden repeated the lines in his head. Magic fades, light bringer returns. He was now absolutely sure Renya's appearance here wasn't just mere chance. She belonged here. The magic marking her was indeed from this world. He questioned who her aunt really was. He doubted she was human. Grayden wondered how to break this all to Renya. She was so strong, but this...to learn you're part of a prophecy and your fate has been predestined? She didn't belong to the world she thought she did. He wished he could shoulder the burden for her. He knew how it felt to have more responsibility than anyone should possibly have.

"You see my prince? There is hope for our kingdom after all! We just have to wait for the appearance of this light bringer!" Almory said, incredibly pleased by his discoveries.

"Almory, you better sit down..." Grayden said, and began to tell the tale of their journey and what he had learned about Renya.

When he'd finished, Almory looked practically delighted. "I'm sure this is the girl the prophecy speaks of. But I'll have to meet her and search her power reserves before I can get a definitive answer."

Grayden nodded. "I'll ask her to my chambers once she's had some rest. The journey was hard, and we were attacked by tygres."

Tumwalt's eyes turned wide. "On our borders?" he asked, dumbfounded.

"I'm afraid so," Grayden said, turning toward Almory. "Speaking of, do you have any healing ointment? I managed to injure myself out there."

Almory fiddled around one of the dusty cabinets against the far wall before pulling out a small blue-colored jar.

Grayden lifted his shirt and removed the wrapping. Tumwalt gasped. "My lord..." he trailed off.

"That bad, huh?" Grayden said, the corners of his mouth moving into a slight grin. "Renya stitched me up."

"Well, she did a surprisingly good job," Almory said, dabbing the ointment on the wound.

"Nothing surprises me about Renya," Grayden replied.

Chapter Twenty

R enya followed Doria through the corridors of the lodge. The halls were covered in a light, warm wood and there were fires blazing in almost every room. She thought it would be cold and drafty, but Snowden Lodge was warm and welcoming.

Doria stopped right outside of a door on the second floor and opened it. Renya stepped inside. The first thing that struck her was how light it was. Five floor-length windows covered one side, and the brightness from the snow shined into the room. A fire was burning in one corner, a gorgeous marble mantelpiece surrounding it. On the other side of the room, there was a huge four-poster bed with the softest white blanket Renya had ever felt. She ran her fingers over it before she explored the rest of the room. She couldn't wait to be beneath those covers tonight. She would never again take an actual bed for granted.

Doria disappeared to a room off to the side, and Renya heard water running. She followed Doria, and smiled when she saw a huge copper tub in the middle of the bathroom, steam already rising in swirling little circles. Doria was dropping bits of oils and herbs into it as the water rose.

"Some lavender and other herbs to help with sore muscles," she said, winking at Renya. "You walk like you've been on a horse for too long."

Renya smiled at her thoughtfulness. "That's so kind, thank you."

"No need to thank me, Mistress Renya. You are the prince's personal guest. If you need absolutely anything at all, I would be happy to assist you. Now you settle down in your bath, and I'm going to go look for some suitable clothes for you. Are you injured anywhere? I see blood on the corners of your sleeves."

Renya explained their attack. Doria looked impressed when she told how she had patched Grayden up.

"I'm most grateful you returned our prince in one piece," Doria said. "We are all quite fond of him."

"I'm beginning to feel quite fond of him myself," Renya said without thinking. She instantly regretted it and blushed in embarrassment.

Doria just smiled her kind smile and went out the door.

Renya wasted no time stripping and submerging herself into the large tub. The hot water soothed her muscles and the rising steam curled the ends of her hair. She found a variety of little jars that looked to be soaps. Renya washed her body, feeling more like herself as she rinsed off the evidence of their attack. She couldn't imagine what Doria must think of her. She had dried blood underneath her fingernails from pressing on Grayden's wound, trying to stanch the bleeding. Her dress was torn in multiple places and she was certain she smelled like smoke from their fire and even fireale from using it to disinfect her hands.

Renya sighed happily and laid her head against the back of the tub, closing her eyes for a few minutes. It was amazing how good a simple bath could make her feel.

When the water got cold, she found a soft towel and dried herself off before wrapping it around her body. She found a smaller towel and wrapped it around her hair. Renya walked back into the main room and looked for some clothes to change into, but didn't see any. Her borrowed dress from the inn was gone, and Renya guessed Doria took it away to be cleaned. Or maybe burned. It was in pretty awful shape.

Just then, there was a knock on the door. Ah, that must be Doria with some clothing for her. "Come in," she said, stepping away from the bed into the middle of the room, admiring the view out the window.

"I'm so sorry!"

She turned around and saw Grayden in the doorway, with his jaw lowered and his mouth wide open. Renya stood there awkwardly, in nothing but a towel.

"Oh my gosh!" she exclaimed, trying unsuccessfully to cover herself more. "I'm so sorry, I thought you were Doria!"

Grayden turned around to give her privacy, but Renya was sure image of her silhouette must be burned into his mind. She was angry at herself for being so foolish.

"You thought I was a woman?" he asked.

"Yes, she was going to bring me some clothes," she explained lamely.

He cleared his throat awkwardly. "After you are dressed, will you come across the hall?"

"What's across the hall?" Renya asked.

"My rooms. I wanted to have our seer, Almory, meet with you."

Renya frowned. Why did he want her to meet their seer? Perhaps it had to do with opening a portal to get her home? "Of course, just as soon as I'm dressed," she said, reminding him she was only in a towel and therefore not invited to linger.

"Thank you, Renya," he replied, heading back into the hall and securely shutting the door behind him.

The next knock on the door brought Doria with some clothing options for Renya. "I'm afraid you are too tall for Selenia's clothing," she said, shuffling through a few gowns. "But I found these packed away. They belonged to Grayden's mother. You're about the same size, I think."

Doria sat the dresses on Renya's bed and sorted through them, pausing to consider each one before she held out a silk, turquoise colored dress. The material was light and flowing, and seemed much different from the other dresses she had seen women wear thus far. "Are you sure it's okay that I wear this?" Renya asked.

"Of course, the prince won't mind, especially when you are his guest. He has a kind heart."

Doria passed Renya some clean undergarments and she slid them on under the towel. Doria slipped the dress over Renya's head and helped to settle it on her hips before pushing her in front of the large bathroom mirror.

It was the most beautiful dress Renya had ever seen. The top part of the dress appeared sleeveless, but tiny sleeves of tulle hung halfway down her arm with crystal snowflakes embroidered on them, making her arms look bare except for the snowflakes. The front was low cut, plunging halfway down to her navel, but the same snowflake-embroidered tulle subtly covered her skin. Luckily, the skirt was simple and light and clung to her legs when she walked. It fit perfectly and for the first time in her life, Renya felt like a princess. It was an odd sensation, but not wholly unwelcome. She never really had a 'princess stage' growing up, and although her childhood friends donned tiaras and walked around on too-high heels, Renya never did. But in this moment, she truly enjoyed the way she looked.

Doria came up behind her and braided Renya's damp hair. She fashioned a sparkling snowflake clip at the end of the braid and then tucked one in front of her ear. Doria held out a pair of delicate flats which Renya hurried into and then declared her dressed.

"Thank you so much," she said, as Doria closed the door on her way out. Renya looked at herself in the mirror for a few more seconds, admiring the way the clips sparkled in the light. They were so intricate and beautiful. She couldn't tell if they were diamond or crystal, but nonetheless, she loved them.

She opened the door and walked across the hall. Grayden's door was already open and she could hear voices. She walked in and saw Grayden sitting at a desk with two other men surrounding him. They were pouring over a bit of parchment, and she heard the older man mention dragons. Renya recognized the one man as Tumwalt, whom she had met earlier. She deduced the older man must be their seer.

Grayden's bedchamber was similar to hers, but his room overlooked the garden and out at the snow-covered mountain caps. The view was breathtaking, and Renya saw a magnificent white-colored bird fly high in the distance. There was a large rug in the center of the room, and Renya could hear another fire crackling off the main room, where she suspected his bed was located. But what she noticed most of all was the smell. She breathed in, and that masculine, evergreen smell of his body consumed her.

Grayden looked up as she made her way into the room. His eyes met hers, and she suddenly felt more beautiful than she ever felt before in her life. She watched his gaze sweep over her, concentrating on the translucent fabric covering her arms and chest. He took a deep breath, obviously pleased by her appearance, and then gestured for her to sit in the chair across from him.

"Grayden? Did you hear me?" Tumwalt asked.

"Sorry, I was thinking about something else." Renya felt her heart constrict, wondering if the 'something else' was her. She welcomed the thought for just a second, as she watched him stare a little too intently at the parchment in front of him.

"As I was saying, Almory has been our seer for over seventy years. In order to get a reading from you, he needs to hold both your hands. Is that okay?" Tumwalt asked the question to Renya, but looked at Grayden. Grayden nodded curtly.

Almory approached Renya. She smiled nervously as he took her hands. "Nothing to be afraid of, my dear. Just close your eyes and relax." His hands felt wrinkled and the skin thin, but also soft. She gathered that his work was indoors, pouring through books and mixing up strange concoctions. His white hair and beard aged him, but his voice still sounded youthful.

At once, Renya felt a surge go through her. Warmth radiating from her neck fluttered through her to her fingers and toes. She felt something strange and foreign course through her, like a hot beam moving with no pattern, free within her body. Images that she thought she had seen in a dream before flashed through her eyes. A room filled with sunlight. Someone looking down at her? Sparkling blue eyes like hers. A mural, maybe? Sun and stars? And then being torn away from the light, then nothing but darkness and wind. Almory released her hands, and the sensations and visions left her just as quickly as they had come. She tried to grasp them, but they slipped through her mind like grains of sand she couldn't catch.

Almory cleared his throat and paused for effect. "My dear Renya, welcome home."

Chapter Twenty-One

R enya stared at the old man, wondering if he was senile. What did he mean, welcome home? He was obviously off his rocker. She looked around Grayden's chambers and locked eyes with Grayden. Her face paled as she saw the look on his face. He looked at her with an expression of grim determination and...pity? There was also something else clouding his eyes she couldn't read, but she knew it was intense. But there was no shock on his face.

"What are you talking about?" she whispered, as though releasing her voice into the air would make whatever he was about to tell her true.

Almory looked at her, and then at Grayden. He obviously thought Grayden bore the responsibility of telling her.

"Renya," Grayden began at last, "I—we—think you are a descendant of the Sun Realm. Possibly the last."

Renya just gawked at him. He was kidding. He must be kidding her. Any minute now, his lips would curl up and he'd smirk at her and laugh. She waited, but his face seemed to freeze in an aloof expression. He was deadly serious.

"What? How? What are you even talking about?" She glared at the three men. Grayden had a look of sorrow on his face. The other two just watched the interaction between Grayden and Renya, sensing it was best for them not to get involved.

"I believe when you were young, someone brought you to the human world to hide you. I think you're Fae, but someone has put a glamor on you to keep you safe."

"A what? But why? Why would someone do that?" she struggled, trying to make sense of this impossible scenario he was describing.

"They've used magic to permanently alter your features. There is a prophecy about the balance of our lands. Almory spent most of his life searching for the scroll containing it before he came across it in the abandoned recesses of the Sun Realm. He's managed to translate part of it."

"It was unreadable until you arrived in this world," Almory interrupted. "It wasn't until you came that the guardian spell unlocked and I was able to decipher it. Whomever enchanted it didn't want anyone to find out about you until you were already in this world."

"And what does it say?" Renya asked. Her voice wavered as she tried to suppress the surge of fear that came over her.

Grayden recited what Almory had translated so far. The words burned into her mind.

"But surely...I'm not this light bringer. I mean, Renya has to be a common name. I'm sure lots of people carry the name. You yourself said it was an old Fae name that must have been brought into the human world..." she trailed off, looking at Grayden. Instantly, something clicked into place. He already knew. He knew from the moment she'd arrived that she was important. That was why he helped her. Had kept her safe. He wasn't noble or righteous, he was going to use her. Trap her in this land and make her save his kingdom.

Suddenly, she felt violently ill. Everything he told her until this point had been a lie. Not wanting to look at any of them a moment longer, she stormed out of the room and ran back across the hall. She slammed the door shut, collapsed on the bed and tried to hold in her tears, but it was like holding back a dam about to burst.

A desperate knock sounded on the closed door. "Renya!" Grayden pleaded through the door. "Please, let me in so we can talk. You must be confused, and I want to help you—"

Renya opened the door and stood there, simmering with anger. She hoped he could feel the anger radiating just underneath her skin.

"Oh, so have you come to use me? Keep me as a prisoner so I can save your kingdom?" She hissed at him through clenched teeth. "Or perhaps you're hoping to make an advantageous match and marry me off to some skeleton in the Shadow Queen's closet? You can save yourself and marry some dream girl and send me away to a monster."

"Renya, you're talking nonsense," he said, closing the door behind him. She watched the door close, looking anywhere but at Grayden.

"Ah, so it is to be imprisonment then," she said, moving towards the bed. "Have you come to take me and sample me before you lock me in this room?" she spat out at him.

In a split second, Grayden was before her, grasping her upper arms and pressing his warm body into hers. "Trust me, little light bringer," he whispered seductively in her ear, "all I have wanted to do since I found you in the forest was to take you and make you mine." He moved his hands up and down her arms slowly, caressing and touching, both rough and reverent at the same time.

Renya trembled in fear at the harshness of his voice and the passion threatening to overcome him. Anger raged throughout her...but then there was something else. Desire. It coursed through her until it nearly boiled over. Renya hated him...but she needed him in a way she had needed nothing or anyone before.

Without warning, Grayden pulled her face against his and kissed her, desperate and deep. She responded in kind, pushing her lips to his and wrapping her arms around his neck. She tried to stop herself. She was mad, and angry...but she couldn't help but give in to the chemistry between them.

Instantly, her skin felt alive and warm. She felt dizzy, like she might pass out, but her mind kept her upright and in Grayden's arms. He opened her mouth gently with his and deepened the kiss. She met his tongue with hers and a fire ignited within her.

His hands reached up to cup her face, and he bent her towards the bed behind her. He kissed up and down her neck before holding himself on top of her. Renya felt the moisture pool between her thighs as she felt his hard arousal against her leg. She arched her back as he ran his hand along one of her breasts. His fingers came up to push a stray lock of hair away from her face, and then he continued his exploration of her body. His hands felt warm like they always had, and every touch made Renya feel more alive, like she had been asleep for her entire life, waiting to be awoken by this man.

The clips in her hair dug into the back of her scalp as Grayden pressed her into the mattress with his weight. She pulled them off and threw them on the bed next to her and lifted her lips to continue their kiss. Grayden's eyes moved to the snowflake clips, and he paused, his eyes clouding over like a dark storm on the horizon. Before Renya realized what was happening, he had quickly rolled off of her, breathing heavily and laying next to her on the bed. She could see him struggling to calm his breathing and suppress his desire to reach for her again as he raised his hand, only to bring it back down beside him.

"Renya, I'm so sorry," he said, sitting up. His face was flushed, and the lust was still in his eyes. "I don't know what came over me." He grabbed her hand and pulled her up to sit next to him, careful to avoid touching her anymore than he had to.

Renya struggled to speak. Her desire was still raging through her body and something about the response felt so natural. She looked over at the hair clips he was still staring at. He sat there on the bed, with his head hung low and his hands on his thighs.

"Grayden, what is it?" She was still deeply hurt by his betrayal but confused about this kiss and then his sudden withdrawal from her. She could tell that he was as desperate as she was for whatever was happening between them...wasn't he?

He gulped, but didn't meet her eyes. "Those clips... they were a present for my mother. It was the last gift I ever gave her," he whispered.

Renya looked at the bed where Grayden's final gift to his mother lay. She carefully gathered the ornate hair clips, glimmering in the bright light of the room. She held them out to Grayden, palm open, uncertainty in her eyes. He reached out and slowly closed her fingers over the clips and kissed her knuckles softly. He plucked the glittering snowflakes out of her hand and placed them back in her hair.

"They are yours, sweet Renya," he muttered, playing with her braid in between his fingers. "I wouldn't want anyone to have them besides you." He paused, as if realizing he was once again touching her, and drew his hand away.

"Thank you," Renya said, unsure of what else to do. She felt she should refuse them, but the sentiment behind them was far too sensitive a subject.

"I'm so sorry I didn't tell you about my suspicions. There was a moment, that first night on the way back here I tried...I wasn't sure who or what you were. And I didn't know about the prophecy. Almory didn't decode it until after you arrived through the portal. I thought you were important, somehow, to the fate of our world, but I have no intention of keeping you here or keeping the truth from you. I meant what I said; I will find a way to open a portal and get you home." He brought his hand back up to her cheek and raised her face to look at him. "I swear to you, Renya."

Renya's heart fluttered despite her anger. She wanted to believe him. But she had been burned so many times by men who didn't keep their promises. She glanced up at him and the look on his face pained her; he looked like a lost boy, his hair falling messily into his face. Again, she thought of the responsibility he faced every day and the decisions he had to make and live with. How would she have handled the same situation? She wasn't so sure that not telling her was the wrong thing if he wasn't certain.

Grayden stood and held out his hand to Renya. She hesitated, then grabbed it and rose to her feet.

"Will you join us for dinner? I'd love for you to meet Selenia." He pushed his brown hair out of his eyes and he looked so vulnerable to Renya, like her refusal might break him.

"Perhaps," she replied carefully. She was still angry. She once again opened herself up to trust someone, only to be hurt again. She thought about running and trying to find a way home herself. Could she manage it? Was staying here and getting closer to Grayden the best strategy? Or should she take her chances and sneak out while everyone slept?

After Grayden shut the door behind him, Renya went to the bathroom to wash the tears from her face. She looked in the mirror and her own blue eyes stared back at her. Who was she? Was she Renya, the journalist? Renya, the rumored home wrecker? Renya, the light bringer? She didn't know. She always felt so sure of who she was. Even in the past, when the stories came out about her, she still knew who she was, even if the world didn't. But now? She ran her fingers along her rounded ears. She didn't have Fae ears like the others. Maybe they were wrong. Maybe this whole thing was a mistake and they'd realize she was just plain old Renya, a broke, unemployed twenty-four-year-old living above a coffee shop.

There was a knock at the door and Doria strolled in the room.

"I'm here to see if you need anything before dinner —" she started. "Your dress! It's all wrinkled! Fates, how did you do that?"

Renya tried to come up with an excuse that didn't involve rolling around on the bed with their prince, but just stared at Doria blankly. "I'm sorry."

"Oh well, don't fret, I have others here," Doria said, opening the wardrobe where she stashed the other gowns.

"I'm not sure I'm going to dinner. Could you make me a tray? Or show me where the kitchen is?"

"Nonsense!" Doria said, looking surprised. "Selenia has been talking non-stop about the mysterious girl her brother brought home. She's sorely lacking friendship. If nothing else, give the poor girl someone beside her brother to talk to."

Renya gave in.

Within a half hour, she was fixed up and heading down to the dining hall. Renya descended the grand wooden staircase, trying not to trip on her gown. If she was going to be stuck here for any amount of time, she needed more practical clothing. While absolutely gorgeous, she had trouble moving in the wine-red dress Doria laced her into. It was tight-fitting and hugged all of her curves. It was also quite daring, plunging low in the back. Doria had brought out a handsome pair of ruby earrings and studded barrettes, but Renya insisted on wearing the snowflake clips Grayden gifted her. Doria gave her a knowing smile but said nothing as she fastened them in her hair. Renya ignored Doria's look. She liked them, that was all. Or at least, that's what she told herself.

One attendant led her to the dining room, and she stepped inside. There was a glittering chandelier over a large rectangular dining table. The chandelier was made up of tiny crystals resembling icicles hanging down, catching the light from the twin fireplaces sitting on each side of the room. The walls were a bright white with cream-colored wooden scrollwork holding up tiny pillars around the edges. A silver rug lined the floor, and abstract images of snowflakes, polar bears, and spotted eagles decorated it.

Grayden sat in the middle of one of the longer sides of the table, with an empty spot next to him. There was a red-headed girl on his left that looked around eighteen. Renya smiled to herself. This must be Selenia, Grayden and Phillippe's younger sister.

Renya moved further into the dining room, and she could feel Grayden's eyes on her. Deciding she'd rather sit away from him, she started towards the opposite side of the table and away from the middle. Before she could sit down, she heard Grayden's strained voice.

"Renya," he said, looking at her with pleading eyes. "Please, come sit next to me and my sister."

Renya ignored him. She was still angry with him, but also unsure of where they stood after their passionate kiss in her room. If he hadn't stopped them, she wouldn't have. She couldn't believe herself. She hardly knew this man.

Selenia smiled warmly at Renya as she approached the empty spot on the other side of Selenia. As soon as she sat down, Grayden stood up and moved to sit on her other side. Selenia's eyes laughed at her brother's antics, but she didn't say anything. Renya refused to acknowledge him.

"So you must be Selenia," Renya said. "It's so nice to meet you."

"It's nice to meet you too," Selenia said. Her voice was sweet and melodious. She wore her hair down, and the scarlet ringlets framed her heart-shaped face. Her skin was incredibly fair and pale, yet she didn't look unwell or ill. Instead, it seemed to almost sparkle like her dancing eyes. "I'd wondered when my brother would finally bring a girl home. I'd started to wonder if he and Tumwalt were an item."

Grayden choked on his wine. Selenia just smiled

sweetly at him.

Renya instantly liked Selenia. "No, he is just helping me, as long as it suits his needs."

Selenia looked puzzled and Grayden sighed audibly.

"Really?" Selenia raised an eyebrow. "Because I can smell his magic all over you."

Grayden cleared his throat uncomfortably. "Because Selenia doesn't use her magic, it's enhanced some of her other...senses. She knows when there are cakes being made in the kitchen by smell alone, and she knows wherever I go by sniffing after my magic. No matter how hard she begs you, never let her trick you into playing a game of chance. Her eyesight is the sharpest of anyone in this castle. And if you have a secret to tell, make sure she's not anywhere around or it won't be a secret for long."

"Your magic smells like an old man," Selenia mumbled under her breath.

Grayden looked annoyed, but ignored her comment.

"There's so much I don't know about magic," Renya said, looking at Selenia. Grayden tried to catch her eye, but she quickly focused on the girl next to her.

"I can sense you have magic of your own," Selenia said, frowning. "But...it's cloudy. Not faded, like Grayden's, but muted somehow. As if someone painted gray over a colorful masterpiece."

Grayden looked at Renya thoughtfully. "I can sense it too, but it feels...warm to me."

Selenia glanced between the two of them and raised an eyebrow, but said nothing.

Just then, four servers came in with steaming

trays. Renya's mouth watered as she looked at the food placed before her. How long had it been since she'd had a hot meal? Even before coming through the portal, she'd been surviving off of granola bars and popcorn.

Renya loaded up her plate full. There were carrots, meat, potatoes, breads, olives, and cheeses...everything tasted amazing. She sighed happily and ate with relish while Selenia told stories about her and Grayden's childhood.

"And then, our father made both Grayden and Phillippe round up all the livestock," Selenia finished, recounting an episode in which the two brothers had let loose all the cattle into the village.

Renya laughed, enjoying all the tales. Once Phillippe recovered, she hoped to get to know him too. She wished she had grown up with siblings. A jolt hit her, and she realized maybe she had siblings. Or maybe her parents were still alive. If it was true, and she was from this world, why did her parents give her up? And who was Aunt Agatha, really? She bit her lip as the anxious thoughts swirled around in her head.

"Renya?" Grayden asked tentatively. "Are you okay?"

"I'm just feeling really confused right now," she answered honestly.

He reached for her hand on the table and covered it with his. The warmth from his hand made her body tingle. She wanted to pull her hand away, but for reasons she couldn't understand, she let him comfort her.

"That's completely understandable, Renya. Would you like to get some air?"

Renya thought for a moment, and then nodded. Maybe this would be a great time to interrogate him and see if he had any type of concrete plan for getting her home. Grayden pulled out her chair for her. He gave Selenia a quick peck on the cheek and then guided Renya out of the dining room, his arm linked in hers.

He walked her through the hall and down to a set of polished double doors. He grabbed a charcoal colored fur off of a hook near the doors and wrapped it around Renya's shoulders. His hands lingered a bit as he pinned it in place along the hollow of her throat. He pushed open the double doors and held them for her as she followed him out.

Tiny snowflakes whirled around them, never quite seeming to fall. "How do the snowflakes do that?" she asked Grayden. "They just seem to hang in the air."

"I think it's a difference in our air and wind," he explained. "They do eventually fall, but it takes longer."

She nodded, and they walked along a gravel path that seemed to take them just along the outskirts of a small forest, the tall mountains behind them. There were fruit trees and flowering trees, bushes and shrubs. Renya even spotted a few vegetables growing, almost completely covered in a blanket of snow. They walked along quietly, and Renya breathed in the crisp air. A small white animal resembling a chipmunk quickly darted up a tree. They came upon a small marble bench and Grayden sat down, motioning for Renya to sit next to him. Framing the bench were fruit trees, heavy with pale green fruit.

"I can't believe you have fruit in the winter."

"It's winter here all the time, Renya. Our crops are adapted and suited for the land." He reached behind him and pulled a piece of fruit from the tree. The branch gave brief resistance, and a small cloud of snow swirled around his face before landing in his hair. He brushed the snow off of the green fruit and passed it to Renya. She held it in her hands and took a small bite.

"Arctic pears," Grayden said, watching her lips move as she tasted the fruit.

"It's good," she said. "Cold, but good."

"Are you warm enough?" He moved a bit closer to share his body heat. Renya felt a flash of panic ripple through her at having him so close. She was still mad at him, still unsure of his motives, but nonetheless sank into his warmth. She released a small sigh.

"Be honest with me, Renya. Are you okay?"

Right now, with him next to her and the quiet and peacefulness surrounding them both, she felt okay. But she knew when she went back inside and was alone in her borrowed bedchamber, her thoughts would plague her. "It's a lot to take in. I thought I knew who I was and now I'm not sure."

Grayden nodded. "I imagine it's quite a shock. But Renya, you are still the same person. You're still the fiery, independent, stubborn, strong, intelligent woman who I have come to respect and admire."

She glanced up, moved by his words.

"All the things that make you who you are, they are still there. Deep down, you'll always be Renya. Whether you decide to stay in the world you were born into or go back to the world you were raised in."

Their eyes met as gentle flurries circled them.

"What if I don't want to be this light bringer?" she whispered into the night air. "What if I'm not strong enough? I'm worried I'll want to go home and you'll stop me."

Grayden took the pear from her and set it next to

him on the bench. He grabbed both of her hands and held them. "Renya, I believe you can do anything you want. I promise, I will help you however I can, even if it's to send you home. But whatever you decide, I want you to know that you won't be alone. If you go back through your portal, you'll have your aunt. But if you decide to stay here...you'll have me."

She desperately ached to know how she would have him. Would he teach her about magic? Would they thwart the Shadow Queen together? Would they be friends? Or...would they become more? For the first time since coming to his world, she opened her eyes and envisioned the life she might have if she stayed. Renya looked into his eyes, and she saw truth and honesty there.

Renya opened her mouth to speak, but at that moment, several snowballs struck Grayden in the chest. He sat, stunned for a few seconds, and then looked back towards the lodge.

"Selenia!" Grayden roared, and Renya could hear a giggle from somewhere above. Grayden rose and strode back to the lodge and Renya followed, struggling to keep up with his large strides. Before he could get out of the garden, another snowball caught him in the face. He laughed, and then scooped up a gigantic ball of snow and lobbed it as far as he could towards the balconies of the lodge.

"You got me in the crotch, you wanker!" came a male's voice from the balcony. "My balls are gonna freeze off!"

"Jurel," Grayden sighed to Renya. "I told you Selenia was becoming a bad influence on him." He tried to look annoyed and stern, but Renya could see he was enjoying himself. Behind all that responsibility and seriousness, he was still just a young man. A young man who was forced into being something he wasn't ready for. They had that in common, at least. But whereas Grayden had risen to the challenge and accepted his fate, Renya was scared to accept hers.

The snowball fight ceased, and Selenia and Jurel disappeared from the balcony. Grayden escorted Renya back to the doors and they stepped inside, warming their hands by one of the larger fireplaces.

Grayden gently unpinned the cloak from Renya's shoulders and hung it back up. "Can I escort you back to your room?"

"Well, considering it's right next to yours, it would be most insulting if I said no," she teased him.

He placed her hand on top of his arm and led her back up the stairs. The lights were dimmed, and Renya began fidgeting as they moved along the quiet corridor. She became suddenly aware that they were both alone. Why did this feel like a date? It wasn't like he was going to walk her to her door and kiss her goodnight, was he? She pushed the thought away as she turned to face Grayden.

"Well...I guess this is goodnight," she said awkwardly and hated herself for stalling at her door, just like in every single romantic comedy she'd ever seen.

"Indeed, it is."

They both stood there.

All at once, they reached for each other, their mouths meeting desperately. Renya melted into the embrace, giving into the tension that had been building all day.

Grayden's hands traced small circles along Renya's uncovered back and she gasped. Her eyelids fluttered as his fingers traveled further down to her lower back, playing with the laces holding the dress together. Renya ran her fingers along his chest, careful to avoid his injury, mirroring the same patterns he was drawing along her back. His shirt was still wet from the impact of the snowballs, and she longed to remove it and warm his flesh with her lips.

He kissed her a bit harder, breathing into her mouth. "Ask me to stop, Little Fawn," he said, pulling her bottom lip into his mouth and sucking on it gently before releasing it.

"Don't stop," she begged, moaning. His hand moved down until he reached her backside, and his fingers gripped and massaged as he pulled her body toward him, lining up her hips with his. For the second time that day, she could feel his hard member straining against her. He made her feel desirable, something she didn't think possible anymore. Back in her world, she felt tainted by her association with the senator.

"Tell me to leave," he panted, grinding slightly against her.

"Never leave," she pleaded, her hips matching his rhythm.

"I must stop," he groaned, frustrated but still not ceasing the movement of his lips against hers.

She tore her lips from his. "Do you want to come into my room?" she asked him, more begging than asking.

"There's nothing I want more in this world, Renya," he said, his voice husky and dark. He slipped the straps of her gown down and caressed her bare shoulders before placing a kiss on each side of her neck.

She felt for the doorknob behind her back and twisted it, opening the door and backing into her room. Grayden followed her in, still kissing and clutching at her, frantic with longing.

"Grayden!" a voice called from down the hall.

He growled against Renya's mouth and pulled away. Selenia marched down the hall towards them.

"What do you want?" he said gruffly, not trying to hide his annoyance.

Selenia approached them and instantly halted. She took in Renya's disheveled dress and the loose hairs falling out of her braid. "Did I interrupt something?" she asked with feigned innocence.

Grayden exhaled heavily, his face ashen, and Renya was still panting.

"No, you didn't," Renya said breathlessly. "I was just saying goodnight." She darted her eyes from Selenia to Grayden and then retreated to hide in her room, closing the door a little too loudly, and then leaning against it for support. Selenia's voice sounded through the closed door. "You know what, Grayden? I really like her."

Chapter Twenty-Two

R enya and Grayden spent all of breakfast trying to avoid eye contact with each other. If Selenia noticed her iciness toward Grayden, she ignored it and chatted to both of them. Renya, for her part, ate her meal in silence. She couldn't help but think of what almost happened last night. If it hadn't been for all the interruptions, she knew they would have taken things a lot farther. Is this what she wanted? To form a relationship with him? Or was he just trying to keep her here so he could use her?

"What boring things are you doing today, Grayden?" Selenia asked, spearing a piece of an arctic pear with her fork.

Grayden was studying a piece of parchment with intense scrutiny when he looked up at her, slight annoyance on his face.

Renya loved the way Selenia pushed Grayden. He was always so serious, worrying over the fate of his kingdom, but she had a way of bringing him out of his deep thoughts. It was refreshing to see him more relaxed, and the weight lifted off of his shoulders, even for just a second. She also enjoyed his annoyance as well, especially since she was still irritated at him for keeping her identity concealed.

"Those 'boring things' are what keep you safe, warm, and with a belly full of sweets," he scolded lightly.

Selenia just scowled and made a face at him as he

went back to his papers. Renya suppressed a giggle at her antics.

"What are you doing today?" Renya asked in earnest. He finally looked up at her, his eyes intense.

"I need to talk to Almory and ride out to some of the nearby villagers. We need more recruits."

"Can I come?" Renya asked him. She had ulterior motives, and hoped he took it as a sign that she had forgiven him. But she really wanted to learn the area better. If he wasn't serious about getting her home, she would figure it out herself and plan for it.

Grayden looked at her, and she could see him struggling with the decision.

Before he could answer, Selenia spoke up. "Renya and I are going to do something else today, so she doesn't want to spend time with you."

Renya met Grayden's eyes and neither spoke.

"What do you think you are going to do?" Grayden asked, not taking his eyes off of Renya.

Selenia looked between them and grinned.

"We are just going to go into the village and do some shopping. I need a couple of things and I want to show Renya around. You don't know how much longer she's going to be with us."

He frowned, his eyes meeting hers again for a split second before she looked down, breaking their eye contact.

"That does sound really interesting," Renya said.

Grayden looked at both women. "Fine, you can go, but only if Jurel goes with you both."

Selenia just scoffed. "I wasn't asking you for permission."

This time, Renya let her giggle slip. Grayden finally

laughed, too.

"Hurry up!" Selenia instructed Renya, "Before he changes his mind."

Renya finished her eggs and rose out of her chair. Grayden stood up to pull out her chair for her, and Selenia rolled her eyes exaggeratedly.

"I see how it is." Selenia turned towards her brother. "You never pull out my chair."

"I do it for any lady," he retorted. "But I don't see any here besides Renya."

This time, Selenia stuck out her tongue behind Grayden's back.

Grayden grabbed his papers, gave Renya a look full of meaning, and then headed out of the dining room.

"Be careful, both of you," he called over his shoulder.

Selenia grabbed Renya's hand and dragged her out after her. "Let's head to my room. You're going to need a warm cloak if we are going to town. You can borrow one of mine."

Renya followed Selenia back to her room. It was on the second floor, but in the opposite direction of her bedchamber and Grayden's. The corridor to Selenia's chambers had the same wooden walls and a decorative carpet runner, but on the walls there were a series of paintings. Renya stopped to admire them. One painting in particular caught her eye. Hanging just at eye level in an ornate pearly frame was a watercolor landscape. Soft, delicate brushstrokes highlighted a calm, snowy backdrop. A clump of trees stood off to the side, and Renya looked closely. In the tree, perched on a branch, was a snowy white owl. An elkten stood regal along a tiny wooden fence in the background, and an arctic fox was in motion, running towards something. Warm sunlight shone on the horizon, bathing everything in a glow.

Selenia stopped her progress through the hall and walked back to where Renya stood. "My mother painted it," she said faintly. "Despite her asking them, my brothers refused to sit for portraits. Phillippe was off training in the fields and Grayden was busy learning all he could from Tumwalt and Father. So she painted this and used the animals to symbolize us. Mother added me in after the fact when I was born. I'm the arctic fox, Grayden is the elkten and Phillippe, the snowy owl. They are our animal guardians. Do you know what those are? Do you have them where you are from?"

"Yes, Grayden told me that his is an elkten. We saw one on our way here, to the lodge. But no, we don't have animal guardians."

"You saw an elkten? Why didn't Grayden tell me? He told me about finding you, and that you came through a portal, but he didn't mention seeing an elkten."

"It was a very eventful trip," Renya said. "I'm sure he just forgot."

"But still...I love animals of all kinds. I can't believe he saw a real one. They used to be common in these parts, but we thought them extinct for the last fifty years or so. That's amazing. What was it like?"

Renya, with her hyperawareness, was able to recall almost every detail, much to Selenia's delight. Selenia hung on every word, listening intently.

"That's it, the next time Grayden or Phillippe go south, they have to take me!" she practically whined.

Selenia pulled Renya away from the paintings. "Let's get going. The sun has been setting so much earlier lately and if it's dark, Grayden won't let me go."

Renya followed Selenia a few more doors down and entered the room behind her. Selenia's view was similar to Grayden's, with the same mountain caps showing, but she had a pleasant view of the garden as well. Renya glanced out onto the balcony and saw an enormous pile of snowballs sitting right outside the glass door. She smiled to herself, remembering the mischief Selenia had been making the night before.

Renya looked around Selenia's room. She wasn't sure what she expected from the teenage girl, but it fit her perfectly. A little bit messy, but brimming with her personality. She had the same marble fireplace that was in Renya's room, but adorning the mantle were little animals carved out of white aspen. Her bed was white aspen as well, with four posters almost reaching the ceiling. Light blue blankets covered the bed along with a warm white fur. There was clothing all over the floor, and a plate of leftover food sat on the desk.

Selenia watched Renya look around her room. "I'm not the tidiest person," she confessed.

"Trust me, I'm not either," Renya said. She walked closer to the fireplace to look at the carved figurines. One of the wooden horses looked so much like Starlia. Renya picked it up, examining it closer.

"Grayden carved that for me," Selenia said. "Phillippe did some of them too."

"You're all so talented," Renya said. "Your mother painted, I've heard that you sing, your brothers can carve wood..."

"Everyone has a skill. It can just take some people longer to find it than others."

Selenia sounded wiser than her age to Renya.

"What do you like doing?" Selenia asked, looking

through her wardrobe.

"I like to write."

"Like stories?" Selenia prompted.

"Sometimes, but mostly news articles. Your brother said you have people who distribute news around the villages," Renya said.

"That sounds really interesting," Selenia said, her head almost disappearing completely inside the wardrobe and her voice muffled. "Do you like to read too?"

"I do. I like all kinds of books," replied Renya.

Selenia pulled out a deep eggplant-colored cloak lined with a warm white fur. "I think this should fit you. It might be a tad short, but it should do just fine for a trip into the village."

Renya took the garment and threw it over her shoulders. She noticed it had an arctic fox pin on it. Renya smiled when she thought of Grayden's pin on the cloak she had worn when first meeting him. She hadn't realized then the special meaning it held for him.

Selenia stood back and looked at Renya in the cape, then nodded her approval. "Let's go!" she said excitedly.

The women headed out to the courtyard and found Jurel. He was leaning against the wall, waiting. When Selenia and Renya approached him, Renya caught his eyes sliding over Selenia's body quickly before meeting her eyes.

Grayden was right, thought Renya. The two appeared to be more than just girl and guard.

Jurel offered his arm to Selenia, paused, and then offered his other to Renya. Renya grabbed it, and they walked arm in arm out of the courtyard.

Almost as though sensing him, Renya looked back and caught Grayden watching her from an upper window, an intense look on his face. She gave a sarcastic little curtsy, mocking him. She turned away, but still felt his eyes on her as they made their way down the winding path.

"How long of a walk is it to the village?" asked Renya.

"Not too long, just five minutes or so." Selenia replied.

Renya looked at Jurel. "How long have you known Grayden?" she asked him.

"All my life," Jurel said. "My father was one of his father's closest friends. We all grew up together. I'm two years younger than he is."

"And a lot more fun," Selenia added.

Jurel smiled at Selenia's compliment. "Grayden has a lot resting on his shoulders," he said, shrugging. Renya thought it was telling that Jurel defended him.

"Yeah, his big fat head," Selenia whispered to Renya. Jurel pretended not to hear her, but Renya swore she saw his lips twitch upwards.

Soon, the gravel turned into cobblestones and they approached the village. Renya couldn't wait to take it all in. When she first saw it on horseback with Grayden, Starlia had been going too fast for her to look properly. This time, she wanted to commit everything to memory.

Despite how cold it was, all the people bustling by made it feel comfortable and safe. There was a tiny town square in the front, with a few fruit trees, benches, and tables. Several older men with white beards were sitting around playing some kind of board game. Renya thought it looked similar to chess, but instead of squares, the board consisted of several concentric circles looping in and out. There were fires burning every few feet in large ceramic bowls and people stopped their shopping to warm their hands before moving on.

Several of the villagers saw Selenia and smiled at her. They looked at Renya with curiosity, but shared their smiles with her too.

Selenia pulled her into the nearest store and told Jurel to stay outside. "This is where I go for all the undergarments that I don't want Doria to know I have."

Renya let out a hearty laugh as she looked around the store. Everything seemed pretty tame to her, but she couldn't help but enjoy Selenia's scheming. She would be a fun ally to have.

Selenia looked around all the tables, excitedly holding things up to herself. Renya took a peek, too. She was currently wearing a white bralette that went down to her navel and some loose, baggy drawers reminding her of men's boxers. She did miss her matching bra and panty sets. For as fun and beautiful as the dresses she had worn were, they were seriously lacking in the underwear department.

Selenia held up a blue bralette and drawers more closely resembling panties. "What do you think?" she asked Renya.

"I love the color," Renya answered. Selenia added them to the pile in her arms.

"So...tell me," Renya said, trying to broach the subject casually and carefully. "What's going on between you and Jurel?"

Selenia grinned. "First, you have to tell me something."

"Okay..."

"Is your relationship with my brother the type where you feel obligated to tell him everything?"

"Nope," Renya said quickly.

"Okay good. Jurel is my best friend. After our parents died, Phillippe and Grayden were so busy. Phillippe had to take command over all of their Father's soldiers and traveled all the time, and Grayden was left with so much responsibility as he tried to adjust to his new role. Sometimes I would go days without seeing either of them. But Jurel...he was always there for me. There were days when he held my hand while I cried. He tried to cheer me up by making me laugh. He'd bring me flowers and little sweets. We had a really good, solid friendship. But over the past year..." Selenia trailed off, not sure how to describe her relationship with Jurel to Renya.

"You've become even closer?" Renya prompted.

"Yes. I love him and I think he loves me too. I know Grayden is worried we are becoming too close, and I'm afraid he's going to reassign him. But I don't know what I would do without him."

Renya chewed her lip thoughtfully. "Selenia, can I give you some advice?"

"Sure..."

"I think you should tell Grayden how you feel. Tell him exactly what you told me. He just wants you to be happy. And it sounds to me like Jurel is what makes you the happiest. It might be weird for Grayden at first, given Jurel is his friend and you're his little sister, but...I think Grayden will understand."

"Really?" Selenia asked.

"Absolutely," Renya replied confidently.

"Can I ask you something now?" Selenia said, holding up another bralette and feeling the lace around the cup. "What's going on between you and my dumb brother?"

Renya knew that was coming. "We're friends. Most of the time," she said simply.

Selenia raised her eyebrows. "Seriously? I told you the truth. I deserve the same," she demanded.

"Alright," Renya conceded. "I'm attracted to your brother."

"But..."

"But I've been hurt before. In the past. I'm guarded. I made the mistake of trusting the wrong man, and I worry that Grayden doesn't have my best interests at heart. But...he manages to slip through my armor anyways. But, I'm not staying here. There's no point in starting something when I'm not going to be here forever. Besides, Grayden said he's not free either. So really, it's hopeless. I don't know what he's feeling as well. Sometimes I think I know exactly what he's thinking, but then he pulls away from me."

"Renya, now can I give you some advice?"

Renya laughed. "I guess it's only fair."

"I think you need to talk to Grayden. Find out what he's feeling too. I can tell he's crazy about you, and not just because I saw you two...expressing your mutual affection in the hall last night."

Renya blushed. "I thought I played it off cool."

"Enhanced hearing and sight, remember?" Selenia said. "I also think you need to figure out if you are going to stay here or not. I know my brother. It might be hard for you to accept, but if he says he is going to get you home, he will. So at some point, you'll have a choice to make."

"I'm going home, with or without his help," Renya said a little too quickly.

"Are you sure you are?" Selenia asked. "You look

so happy when you're with Grayden. I don't know what you've left behind in your own world, but are you willing to leave behind what you might have here?"

"I guess I have some thinking to do."

"Me too," Selenia giggled. "But first, tell me what you think about this one, with the flowers on it." She held out a matching set with bright red and yellow flowers, and Renya nodded her approval.

Selenia picked out a handful of things and convinced Renya to get some things, too. "Grayden won't mind. He never looks at my expenses, anyway. Plus, if he knew we were buying you pretty undergarments he'd thank me." Selenia said encouragingly.

When they were done, bags tightly grasped in their hands, they joined Jurel, who looked incredibly bored and cold standing outside.

"Where to next?" he asked Selenia.

"Should we grab some lunch?" Selenia asked Renya.

"That sounds great," Jurel replied before Renya could answer. She had the feeling he waited around for Selenia a lot.

Selenia led the way to a charming little eatery. It reminded Renya of an old-fashioned English pub. Selenia pushed through the crowd to a little table in the corner. She ordered some drinks and savory meat pies for them all. She didn't even ask what Jurel wanted before she ordered for him. It was clear the two had spent a lot of time together and knew each other well.

The eatery was noisy but full of life. Renya sat back and observed all the people and their interactions with each other.

If I ever go home, I should write a book about

this place, Renya thought to herself. She watched a group of men in the corner drinking and laughing amongst themselves.

"Does Grayden ever come here?" she asked the pair.

"No. He rarely leaves the lodge unless it's to go to a village or check in with Phillippe somewhere. Half the days he forgets to stop for lunch so Doria chases him around with biscuits until he gives in," Selenia answered.

"I really like Doria," said Renya.

"She's been taking care of all of us since we were babes. Once I turned sixteen, I was expected to get my own maid, but Doria is more like a mother to me. There was no way I was going to replace her. She doesn't clean up after me much anymore, but it's worth it to have her around."

A teenage boy brought their food over. Selenia had ordered her a lotus apple juice, and it thrilled her to taste it again. Selenia had ordered Jurel a fireale, but Renya noticed he really didn't drink it. She wondered if he had to keep his wits about him around Selenia. She seemed so confident and Renya didn't doubt she could be persuasive and used to getting her way.

They ate their meal in relative silence until Renya heard music playing.

"What's that?" she asked.

"It's the sky lights tonight, I'd forgotten! They must be making preparations."

"Sky lights?" Renya asked.

"Yes, a few times a year we get beautiful green lights that flash across the sky. There's a small festival and everyone gathers to watch them. We have to go!"

"Ah, I bet that's the Northern Lights. We have those in my world too, but I've never seen them."

"I wonder if we can get Grayden to attend the festival too. He hasn't been in ages," Selenia said. "He just falls asleep at his desk with parchment stuck to his ugly face."

"What do they do for the festival?" Renya asked her.

"There's lots of food and wine, music and dancing...and as soon as it's dark, everyone watches the lights. Some people even wish upon them. They say 'if you wish under a green wave, your wish will soon be made.' It's a childish nursery rhyme, but I still make a wish every time."

"That sounds amazing," Renya said, taking a last bite of her meat pie and popping an olive into her mouth.

"Let's head back to the lodge and ask Lord Grumpy if he wants to attend." Selenia grabbed Renya's hand and pulled her out of the eatery and back towards the lodge, Jurel trailing behind, carrying Selenia's parcels.

When they reached the lodge, Selenia dragged Renya from room to room, searching for Grayden. They finally found him down in the workrooms, studying a scroll with Almory.

Grayden had his nose practically pressed down to the parchment, while Almory sprinkled a dark powder over it. Renya watched the powder absorb into the parchment as soon as it touched.

"What are you two conjuring?" Selenia asked.

Grayden looked up at the two women. "Just studying the prophecy." He quickly changed the subject. "So, how was the village? What did you think, Renya?"

"It's beautiful and full of life."

"Just like you," he said, and Renya blushed while Selenia made gagging noises. Almory, on the other hand, didn't even seem to notice they'd entered his workshop.

"Did you know it's the sky lights tonight?" Selenia asked Grayden.

He frowned. "No, time has gotten away from me, I'm afraid. Almory, do you need me for anything further? I'd like to escort Selenia and Renya to the Sky Light Festival tonight."

Almory gave a wave of his hand, effectively dismissing them.

"I thought that was going to take a lot more convincing," Selenia said, nudging Renya in the ribs. "He likes you more than I thought."

Renya shushed Selenia as they followed Grayden back up the stairs.

"What time did you want to head to the festival?" Grayden asked when they reached the top of the landing.

"We need an hour. It's non-negotiable," Selenia replied, sensing that her brother would argue.

Grayden laughed. "Fine, I'll meet you both at the great hall in an hour. If you're late, I'll leave without you," he threatened Selenia.

She grabbed Renya's hand and pulled her up the stairs. Rather than head to her room, she started off in the direction of Renya's.

"What are we doing?" Renya asked.

"We are going to get you ready for your first Sky Lights Festival," she said, practically giddy.

Chapter Twenty-Three

The pair entered Renya's room and Selenia went straight for the wardrobe. Before Renya could say anything, Selenia was pulling out gowns and tossing them on the bed.

"No...too red. Bleh! Seriously, does anyone wear orange anymore...too casual...ah ha!" She pulled out a midnight blue dress from the very back of the wardrobe.

It was simply cut, with a full skirt and tulle sleeves that fell off the shoulder. The neckline plunged further than Renya was comfortable with, but the skirts caught her eye. Silver snowflakes and dark blue stars adorned the entire skirt, the crystal beading radiating in the light. The bodice was a simple velvet in midnight blue, with a bit of gold filigree trimming the waist. It looked exactly like the night sky in the Snow Lands. Renya wanted to refuse it, since it was far too formal than anything she'd ever worn and she didn't even think the skirts would make it through the door. However, the sheer beauty of the dress took her breath away and brought her back to images of prom. She'd never gone to a prom and had never worn a ballgown.

Selenia watched her as she appraised the gown. "I know, it's perfect," she told Renya.

"Are you sure it's not too formal?"

"No, it's fine. I'm going to wear something similar. Here, put it on."

Renya went over to the bathroom and slipped off the relatively simple dress she had worn to the village. She stepped into the gown and slipped it up over her chest.

"Are you almost done?" Selenia asked.

Renya glanced in the mirror before walking out. It was the prettiest dress she'd ever seen. Renya had never been into fashion, but she knew this gown was special.

Selenia squealed. "You look amazing!"

Renya turned her back to Selenia so she could help lace up the back.

Selenia was pulling the dark blue satin laces up the back when Doria entered the room.

"I've come to see if you need help dressing for—" she stopped short when she saw Renya in the gown. "Oh my, you look absolutely radiant, Renya."

"I know!" Selenia said excitedly, as if it were her Doria complemented. She finished lacing Renya's dress and then stood back for the full effect.

"My brother won't be able to take his eyes off of you tonight." She smiled broadly and then disappeared out of the room to change in her chambers.

Doria came closer to admire the dress. "I'm assuming you want to wear the snowflake clips again?"

Renya nodded, and Doria started twisting Renya's hair into intricate braids. When she was finished, she tucked the snowflake clips in and then went to the wardrobe. She came out with a pair of satin shoes. Renya slipped them on and then tried to pull on the cloak Selenia had loaned her.

Doria stopped her. "Wait to put it on until after he sees you."

Renya thought it was telling she didn't even need

to call Grayden by name. Was their flirtatious behavior so transparent?

She looked in the mirror again while Doria bustled around the room, picking up the dresses Selenia had scattered about.

"I can always tell where Selenia's been," Doria sighed with a smile.

Renya chuckled. "Are you coming to the festival?" she asked Doria.

"I might. The cold tends to make my bones ache, but I'll try to catch a bit of it. You enjoy yourself, Renya."

"Thanks," Renya said, heading out of the room. She was glad when she found out she could, in fact, leave the room with the enormous skirts.

She walked along the long corridor and down the stairs. The gown seemed to float with every movement she made. She took the stairs carefully, not trusting herself to make it down unscathed. At least the satin slippers were flats, she thought to herself.

With her nerves buzzing, she walked into the great hall. Grayden had his back turned, looking into the fire crackling in the fireplace. He caught her movement out of his peripheral vision and turned.

Renya worried the gown was too much, but Grayden's look told her she'd worried for nothing. His eyes were wide, and he had a far off smile on his face as his eyes drank her in. It took a few seconds for him to say anything, and Renya felt a brief rush of pride at rendering him speechless.

"You look...there isn't even a word to describe how perfect you look," he finally said.

"Thank you," Renya said, looking at him. Unlike the usual tunics he wore around the lodge, Grayden had donned a black button-up overcoat with dark gray trousers. His boots were polished, and he was freshly shaven. He held out his arm to her, and she took it. Renya was glad to see that despite his formal attire, his dark brown hair was still untidy. She liked how it made him look younger and less serious. She ached to push it back and feel the soft curls again.

"Here I come!" a voice bellowed from the top of the stairs as Selenia announced her own arrival.

Renya and Grayden both turned to see her descend the stairs gracefully. She wore a lavender gown with white evening gloves that went up to her elbows. Grape-colored amethyst stones sparkled around her throat.

"You look beautiful, Selenia," Grayden said as she reached the bottom of the stairs. He held out his other arm to her, but at that moment Jurel came in from the opposite door and Selenia ignored her brother. She raced to Jurel and stood in front of him, grinning. Jurel, for his part, wore his regular guard uniform, but Selenia didn't even seem to notice or care.

Renya could tell at once Selenia's feelings towards Jurel were reciprocal. Jurel looked at Grayden's sister with warmth and affection. He whispered something to her, and she grinned.

Grayden frowned at their interaction, but Renya caught his eye and gave him a knowing look. She'd have to intervene on the couples' behalf at some point. But not tonight. Tonight, she wanted to enjoy the festivities.

With Renya tucked close to Grayden and Selenia on Jurel's arm, they headed into the village.

Chapter Twenty-Four

Grayden couldn't take his eyes off of Renya as they made their way carefully down the hill towards the center of the village. His heart had stopped when he saw her walking towards him in the great hall. He had never seen a more beautiful woman in his life. He thought he recognized the dress as his mother's, and he was surprised how touched he felt seeing Renya in it. She was regal, looking down at him with a shy smile on her face. He had returned her smile softly and urged his breathing to slow. For Fate's sake, he was a grown man with a kingdom to rule and instead, he was panting over a girl like a young boy. He quickly shook his head before the thought overcame him. He looked ahead at the path, the streetlamps bright and cast a warm glow before them.

Renya stopped for a second to adjust her cloak, and Grayden hung back with her, allowing Jurel and Selenia to go on ahead of them. She fiddled with Selenia's arctic fox pin on the borrowed cloak before Grayden pulled it from her fingers gently.

He removed the elkten pin off of the front of his overcoat and tucked Selenia's pin in his pocket to give back to his sister later. Standing before Renya, he brought the edges of the cloak together and secured them with the representation of his animal guide.

"I want you to wear mine," he said, trying to claim her as his for the moments they had left together.

Renya smiled shyly at him, warmth creeping up her neck.

They started back along the path and into the village square. Grayden felt oddly nervous, but he wasn't sure why. Perhaps it was just because of how beautiful Renya looked. She looked so alluring that he had to bury the burning need he felt to claim her in more primitive ways. Grayden cared very little for dresses and gowns, never really noticing what women adorned their bodies with, but seeing Renya covered in snowflakes, the sign of his lands, made him desperate for her. It touched him that she continued to wear the clips he gave her. Grayden thought of his mother and wondered what she would have made of Renya. He imagined they would get along well. He sensed Renya longed for family, and his mother had so much love to give. Grayden was sure she'd feel Renya should have the diamond clips, too.

They approached the square and Grayden caught Selenia trying to force-feed Jurel a sweet cake. He didn't know what he was going to do about those two. He'd have to bring it up with Phillippe. Grayden wondered how his brother was doing. He was eager for him to return so they could dive into strategizing. But he could worry about that tomorrow. Tonight, he wanted to spend one carefree evening with Renya.

Renya's eyes were darting, trying to take everything in. Grayden pointed out some of his favorite stalls and mentioned the things he liked to do as a child.

"We have to get a dipped lotus apple," he said. "They cover it with clotted cream and sprinkle it with cinnamon."

"Sounds good to me," Renya said as Grayden led her over to a stall. The people who passed gave Grayden polite bows of the head or tipped their hats as he passed by, but for the most part, they allowed him space. He caught several people glancing at Renya, and he knew Tumwalt would be unhappy about having to squash rumors about her tomorrow, but he didn't care. Let them gossip. For one night, he wanted to be happy and pretend he had a real future ahead of him, instead of the sacrifices he saw himself making for his lands and his people.

Grayden paid the vendor for the apples and found a spot for them to sit by one of the ceramic fire pits. Renya had trouble adjusting her voluptuous skirts, but eventually she just pulled them to one side.

"Don't worry. If they wrinkle, Doria will know how to get them right again."

"I know, when they were wrinkled the other day from when we, I mean, when I..." she trailed off awkwardly.

Grayden knew she was referring to the incident in her room and he desperately wanted to talk to her about it, but he was terrified. He knew Renya wanted to return home, but hearing her say it would cause him pain. He didn't know how long she would be with them, and he couldn't think about her leaving without despair filling his heart. He meant it when he said he was going to find a way to open a portal for her. He had already started discussing with Almory how to go about it. Both Almory and Tumwalt didn't understand his decision to pursue opening a portal for her. Not only did they think he should keep her here because of the prophecy, but opening a portal would drain Grayden's magic and leave their people and lands susceptible. Grayden knew what he promised her might be the wrong choice for his people, but he would never go back on his word. Not even after learning about the prophecy.

"So, did you enjoy spending time with Selenia earlier today?" he said, eager to get his mind off the thought of her leaving him.

"I did! We went shopping and had some lunch. Everyone in the village seems friendly."

"I'm glad," he said, finishing up his apple and reaching for Renya's apple core to discard it for her. He came back to the bench they were sitting at, and lively music began playing. Several of the villagers joined together and started dancing. On the far end, furthest from where Grayden and Renya sat, he could just make out Selenia dancing a lively jig with Jurel.

He looked at Renya and held out his hand.

She looked at him, shaking her head. "I can't dance. I don't know how, and I swear I have two left feet."

"I'm not sure what that means, but you'll be fine with me, I promise," he said.

Renya grabbed his hand and allowed him to pull her up, skirts floating around her.

Grayden demonstrated some of the basic steps and pretty soon Renya had it down, laughing and spinning with her full skirts twirling around her. The song ended, and then a slower melody played.

He grabbed Renya's waist gently and pulled her body close to his, holding her other hand in his. Grayden swayed with her around the square, his deep voice humming the melody of the song into her ear. He caught Jurel and Selenia dancing close as well, but he couldn't bring himself to care. Not when Renya was in his arms, looking so beautiful and smelling heavenly.

She looked up into his eyes, and he felt the connection between them. He brought his hand up to her cheek, and she leaned into his palm. Grayden felt her flush slightly at his touch, blood pooling in her apple-shaped cheeks. He loved that so damn much. Her hand felt so natural in his, and he intertwined his fingers with hers. It was such an intimate gesture that he expected her to take her hand back, but instead she gave him a little squeeze with her fingers.

The song ended and Renya slowly pulled away. Grayden held her hand and took her over to another stall, getting them each a drink.

Selenia came bouncing over to them, breathless and her cheeks pink. "Should we go find a spot? It's dark enough to see them."

Grayden led them slightly away from the village center. As the darkness of night approached, the two couples lifted their heads to the sky as the lights danced above them. Greens and blues and reds flashed across the sky, moving and shimmering.

"It's like they're dancing," Renya murmured.

Grayden put his arm around her. "Legends say they are the souls of maidens dancing in the sky."

He saw the look of awe on her face and felt his heart surge. He wished he could show her all of the things this world offered. They could climb on Starlia's back and he'd hold her tight as they traveled across the lands. He'd show her the Blue Ice Lake and take her into the Frozen Mountains to see the Ice Falls. Grayden would take her to the tropical reaches of the Tidal Kingdom and they'd look at the cherry blossoms in the Spring Realm. He allowed the dream to enrapture him, but only for a minute. He knew Renya would go back from where she came and he would once again be alone, the responsibility he bore slowly smothering him.

They continued to watch the light play and flash across the midnight sky. As the night got colder, more and more people left the square for the warmth and comfort of their homes.

"Should we head back?" Grayden asked, touching Renya's arm to get her attention.

Renya nodded, teeth chattering. Selenia looked equally cold. Both men held out their arms to their respective charges and they headed back up to the lodge, the pearly translucent lights guiding their way home.

Chapter Twenty-Five

"**R**enya, I'd like to show you something once you've finished," Grayden said.

Renya pushed some fried potatoes around her plate and looked up at him. "Okay," she said, trying to make her voice sound normal and even. Since their dance last night, she suddenly felt shy around him. She was becoming more and more sure of his feelings towards her, and she was beginning to think hers were just as strong. She took a drink and popped another piece of fruit into her mouth and stood up as he pulled out her chair.

Grayden left the dining room and she followed him up to the third level of the lodge. She had never been on this floor before, but it looked similar to the second level. The same wood paneling gleamed in the brightness from the snow outside. A few housemaids passed them in the hall, and Renya could see them glancing bashfully at Grayden while also trying to get his attention. Grayden didn't even seem to notice their flirtatious attempts, much to Renya's relief, but then she scolded herself. She was going home. It didn't matter if the housemaids flirted with him.

Grayden opened a large door and Renya followed in behind him.

It was a library, full of hundreds of thousands of books. The space was bright, with a huge skylight in the roof and warm blonde wood bookshelves lining every space along the walls. In the center were several desks and armchairs, and like every other room in the lodge, a massive fireplace stood in the center, making the room toasty and comfortable.

"This is amazing," Renya gasped as she took it all in. "I love to read."

"I figured you might find some entertaining books in here, but I actually brought you here for a different reason." He walked over to the far side of the wall to a collection of extremely old books. Books of every color and size caught her eye, some even circular. Every third book seemed to be newer, but the oldest ones were crumbling.

Renya turned her head sideways to look at the spines, but couldn't make out any of the titles. "What are these?"

"They are the history of my people—well, our people," he corrected. "I knew you were feeling lost, trying to figure out who you are, and I thought this might help a bit. It tells about the different realms, magic and famous rulers..." he trailed off.

"How can I read them?" she asked. They looked to be in a Fae language.

"The newer copies are translations," he said, pulling one of the newer books out and handing it to her.

"History of the Spring Lands," Renya said as she read the inside cover aloud. "This is incredible. Thank you."

Grayden didn't say anything for a long moment. Finally, he bent over to the lower bookshelf and pulled out a couple more books and handed them to Renya. "This is what we know about the Sun Realm," he said. "You might find it particularly interesting."

He turned out and walked out of the library, leaving Renya alone with the books. She wished he would have stayed with her; she had become quite accustomed to his presence. Renya imagined the maids in the hall trying to flirt with him and found herself jealous. Grayden hadn't paid them the slightest notice, but it irritated her that they lusted after their attractive prince. Renya knew she had no claim to him, but she was glad that he didn't even seem to notice the women and their attempts.

She turned over the other book he had given her and read the inside cover: Snowden Family, a History. A tiny snowflake was embossed on the cover and gold filigree twirled down the sides of it. Renya opened the book and saw a large family tree spreading over at least thirty pages. She skimmed down to the last page and found Grayden's name and rubbed her finger over the ink announcing his birth. She also noticed powers, or lack thereof, were listed next to each individual. Under Grayden's name and his date of birth, it read 'Elemental Magic'. She wondered what that meant. She looked at his birth date and quickly did the math, comparing it to the strange calendar she saw sitting on one of the tables. If the calendar worked like she thought it did, he was only twenty-four. The same age as her. She went back a generation and found his parent's date of death. Five years ago. He had only been nineteen when he was placed in charge of his realm. She couldn't fathom the amount of pressure he must have on him every day. Yet, he still found time to help her. She knew he said he admired her, but Renya was quickly starting to think highly of him as well. He was patient and kind, brave and sincere. Qualities that surprised her in someone so young. Back in her world, twenty-four-year-old males were still boys, with little responsibility in their lives. Grayden, on the other hand, was a man.

She traced the line back to his parents. Efferon and Elowyn. They were over a hundred each when they died. Time must move differently here, or Fae must live longer. Underneath the line connecting their names together, there were two words. She squinted to read them, the elegant, flowing text hard to decipher. 'Fate-Bonded.' What did that mean?

Renya spent the next couple of hours in the library reading. She read her way through the entire Sun Realm translation, even searching for herself in the family tree. It was no use though. She found no mention of a 'Renya' in the last fifty years, before the lineage abruptly stopped.

A little before midday, Grayden came back into the library. Renya looked up from her current book and smiled at him.

"Are you learning anything interesting?" he asked.

"Do Fae live longer?" she asked, closing the book and pushing it away from her.

Grayden regarded her thoughtfully. "I'm not sure how long humans live. Fae usually live around two hundred years or so."

"Definitely longer than," Renya mused. "What about this comment next to your parents' names?"

"Fate-bonded."

"Yes, what does it mean? I haven't seen it with any of the family trees. Also, it seems like the lines are dying out. Fewer children each generation, many couples without them entirely."

He sighed. "It's all a sign of our fading world, and both are intertwined. You are very astute, Renya."

She waited for him to explain, curiosity in her eyes, but sympathy in her heart at the sound of his sorrow.

"Fated bonds have become incredibly rare over the last thousand years," he said, "and it starts with a legend. When we are created, it is said that for every Fae made, their match was made as well. Their perfect partner in every way. Sometimes the Fates enjoyed separating them, or making the circumstances around finding each other difficult, but most could locate each other. It made things so simple, yet exciting to know that one person was out there somewhere, waiting for you."

"What happened?"

"I'm not sure. No one is. Some say as the magic faded, our ability to sense the bond faded with it. Others think that with fewer children being born, as you noted, Fae are no longer made with a match."

"That's so sad," Renya said. She knew the magic was fading in his lands, but effecting their ability to find love and create families? It was tragic. "So your parents found this bond, though?"

"Yes." Grayden said. "It comes at a different time in each couple's lives. Sometimes they find each other young and are friends for a long time before it turns into something more. But if it develops, it's before the age of twenty."

Renya pursed her lips, deep in thought. There was a lot to learn about this world. Some things seemed so similar to her world, yet there were drastic differences. She wondered if the similarities were enhanced due to the loss of magic in his world, and if day by day, it became more like the human realm as the magic faded.

"And this is what you hope for Selenia? And why

you haven't entertained marriage offers?"

"Yes. I know the chances are slim, but she still has time for a fated bond to claim her heart. Maybe I'm a fool, but I can't take that chance away from her, however slight."

"That doesn't make you a fool, Grayden. It makes you a loving brother. But you should talk to Selenia. See what she wants. She's actually really wise behind her antics."

Grayden scratched his chin. Renya noticed he had shaved again. He looked even younger without the dark stubble. She suddenly had the urge to run her hands along his cheeks, to feel how soft his skin would be without the bit of facial hair. He caught her looking at him and she dropped her eyes back to the stack of books quickly.

He seemed slightly embarrassed talking about Selenia's love life and changed the subject. "Would you be interested in learning how to ride?" he asked, pulling her away from her thoughts.

It took Renya a split second to realize what he meant. "Of course!" she said excitedly. She missed Starlia and wanted to get the chance to see her again.

"I had Doria find you some proper riding attire. She's waiting in your room to get you ready. Shall I meet you outside in the courtyard?"

She nodded, placing the books back on the shelf and then heading down to the second level.

The riding outfit was nothing like anything Renya had seen before. The top was black and long-sleeved, with bits of red trim along the arms. Around the collar, a gorgeous bit of white fur crept up her neck. The pants were a soft black leather, but a red skirt pooled around her legs, with a slit completely up the middle. A pair of supple leather boots and black leather gloves completed the look. After wearing gowns for the last few days, Renya loved the ease of movement the outfit afforded her.

"Did this belong to Grayden's mother?" Renya asked Doria as she braided Renya's hair.

"No," Doria replied, weaving a red ribbon through the braid. She left the snowflake clips on the table. "The prince asked it to be made especially for you. I took some things I had and put this together. He wanted something you could be comfortable in while you learned."

The unexpected gesture surprised Renya, but she wasn't sure why. He had been so kind and generous, with both his time and his hospitality. But picking out clothing for her felt...intimate. A rush of heat went through her. Perhaps on this ride they could talk and she could get to the bottom of what was going on between them.

Renya met Grayden in the courtyard, only to find two strange horses before her.

"Where's Starlia?" Renya questioned, disappointed.

"I didn't think she was in fit condition to ride," Grayden explained. "We just found out we are expecting a foal from her."

"That's wonderful news," Renya said. "Is it her first?"

"That it is. I'm a bit excited too. And now Phillippe owes me. I bet him twenty pieces of gold that Starlia would foal before Necteria." Grayden grinned.

Renya laughed. "How is Phillippe?"

"He's doing much better. We had a messenger this morning. In fact, he might even be on his way here. The Snowden line heals fast," Grayden winked. It was true, Grayden's injury seemed to not be bothering him at all.

"So, which horse is mine?" Renya asked, looking between the two animals. One was gray with a silvery mane, and the other was all white with a gorgeous black mane.

"The white one, Frost, is your mount. She was my mother's horse and she should be tame and polite to you. The gray one is called Lightning. He's fast, but stubborn."

Grayden helped lift Renya onto the light-colored horse. One of the grooms led her out of the courtyard and up a slight hill to where an open plain lay before them.

"Thank you, Joff," Grayden said to the groom. "Would you tell my sister we'll be back before dinner?" He turned to Renya and went over some riding basics with her. She spent the next hour learning to trot, lead, and communicate with the mare. Frost was a sweet horse, but honestly, Renya thought, kind of stupid. Either that or Renya was just a horribly inept rider. Still, Grayden was patient with her, offering gentle corrections. Once he felt she had a grasp of the basics, he suggested they try out an easy trail in the woods. They rode for a little while, the horses' hooves practically silent in the snow.

When they came upon a small stream, they stopped to water the horses. Grayden dismounted and helped Renya off her horse. Unlike all the other times he lifted her off of Starlia's back, he lingered as he held her to his body and slowly lowered her down. Renya could feel the tension in his muscles at his restraint. Her boots hit the soft snow and she looked up at Grayden, her eyes burning with desire. She saw the same look of lust in him as well. But when he didn't seem willing to make the first move, she pressed her body just slightly into the soft circle of his arms. He wrapped his arms around her and just held her, his chin resting on her head. Unlike their hurried and desperate kisses before, Grayden slowly lifted her chin and pressed delicately against her lips with his. His gloved hand went up to caress her cheek, and she leaned into the touch. It felt so good to be touched like this, tender and slow. Grayden let out a contented sigh and deepened their kiss as Renya moaned. He moved her backwards until her back was up against a tree. His mouth moved down to her neck, and he nuzzled and began kissing a hot trail down to her shoulders, moving aside the soft fur of her collar as Renya closed her eyes with pleasure.

"Well, look what we have here."

A man, dressed head to toe in black, appeared from behind a thick tree. He had a well-groomed black beard and his eyes were so dark Renya couldn't make out his pupils.

"Renya, stay behind me," Grayden ordered, and turned to face the man, pulling a small dagger out of his boot.

"Now, now," said the man, "is that how you Snowdens welcome your guests?"

Grayden snarled. "When they set dragons on my men, we don't consider them guests."

The man ignored Grayden's accusations. "And who is this lovely lady? I didn't know you had a lover, Snowden."

Renya would have blushed if she hadn't been so scared. She could feel the malice radiating off of this man.

"Aren't you going to introduce me?" he asked in a sickeningly sweet voice.

"No," Grayden growled in a tone Renya didn't recognize.

"Very well, I'll introduce myself. Renya, I believe I

heard our dear Prince Grayden call you? I'm Brandle, a humble servant of the Shadow Queen's." He gave a little bow, dipping forwards like a puppet on a string.

"Renya, get on the horse and ride to the lodge," Grayden instructed. "Now!"

Before Renya could move, a dark shadow erupted from Brandle's fingertips and crept towards her, engulfing her in darkness and paralyzing her.

"No!" Grayden cried out. "Your queen's quarrel is with me. Release her," he pleaded, helpless against the dark shadow twisting around Renya.

"Now, why would I want to do that? What I want to —"

Before Brandle could finish, a thick sheet of ice rose up in front of Renya, shielding her from the attack. At once, Renya was free from the shadow's grasp.

"Renya, run!" Grayden yelled, gritting his teeth in concentration as he forced every bit of magic he had into holding up the wall of ice protecting her.

She turned and started for the horses. With a loud crack, Grayden's ice shield shattered. Brandle raised his fingers and aimed for Renya again. Grayden jumped in front of her and the shadow went through him, knocking him to the ground. Brandle's magic held Grayden flat on the forest floor as another dark cloud pulled at Renya. She fought, but the shadow held her tight.

Brandle looked down at Grayden, cruel laughter bubbling up from his lips. "How lucky is this! I came to steal away your sister, and instead, I find you with your lover! Tell me, is she your betrothed? Or just some whore you're fucking?"

Grayden was twisting and thrashing hard against the black shadow holding him down. "You touch a hair on her head and I will hunt you down and slit your throat," he spat.

Brandle walked over to where Renya stood, trapped in the black mist. He reached inside and ran his fingers through her braid and pulled out the red silk ribbon Doria had carefully woven into her hair earlier. He brought it to his nose and inhaled deeply. "I can see your fascination with her. She smells heavenly. There's something about her that is so familiar, though. Pity I'm going to have to kill her. But I might at least try her out a bit first. After all, if she can appease your appetite, I'm sure she'll wet mine."

Renya looked at Grayden, frantic. Tears poured down her face and her body trembled in fear. She tried to call out to him, tried to think of something to say to get her out of this mess, but Brandle snapped his fingers and Grayden and the Snow Lands disappeared right in front of her eyes.

Chapter Twenty-Six

R enya woke up with her head pounding. Her cheek was pressed against the cold, hard floor. She opened her eyes, only to be surrounded by near darkness. There was an orange glowing light in the corner. Where was she? More importantly, where was Grayden? She remembered the haunted look in his eyes when Brandle touched her. Grayden was scared, which made her absolutely terrified. Why had this man taken her, and for what purpose? Grayden had mentioned the Shadow Queen. Did she know about the prophecy? Did she know Renya was important to their world, or was it just a random chance the man had found her instead of Selenia? How much did they know about who she was?

Her eyes adjusting, Renya looked around her. She appeared to be in some kind of cell, but there were no bars on the front. The walls were damp to the touch and the light coming from the corner was actually a torch. She stood up, her muscles sore and protesting. Why were there no bars on the cells? Her heart leaped for a second and she ran towards the entrance. She smacked into a hard wall and fell back into the cell. Renya picked herself up, the base of her spine burning from the fall. She moved closer to the opening with her arms outstretched. When she got close, she tried to press her hands through the space. There was nothing physical there, but something was preventing her from leaving.

Magic, Renya thought. Magic sealed her in this dark cavern. She shivered, despite the warm riding outfit she still had on.

"I wondered how many times it would take for you to realize the barrier was invisible," a cruel voice came. "Since you are human, I figured at least three. Pity. I would have enjoyed watching you bounce off the magical barrier a few more times. Plus, the more you're bleeding when your lover gets here, the more—shall we say—agreeable he will be in our negotiations."

Bluffing. Renya knew bluffing might be the only way out of this. "What makes you think he'll come for me?" she said, trying to sound casual. "You picked wrong. I'm nothing to him. Just a fling, a dalliance. You should have chosen someone he actually cares about."

"I knew you were human, but I didn't realize how stupid you must be. Don't lie, girl," he sneered. "I can smell his weak and pathetic magic all over you. He's all but marked you."

Renya pretended to laugh. "I'm sure all his girls smell like him. He won't come for me. He doesn't care for me at all." Her chest constricted, and she fervently hoped Grayden was on his way right now.

"Oh really? Well, let's make a little wager. If he comes for you, I'll kill you in front of him. If he doesn't... well, I'll still kill you but perhaps I'll give you a sporting head start. But not right away. We might have to have a little fun of our own."

Bile rose in Renya's throat. She felt so helpless. After escaping from the senator's attack, she promised herself she would never let herself be in a situation like it again. But here she was, trapped. She had trusted Grayden. He warned her being around him was

186

dangerous, but she still clung to him like a life preserver.

"What, no threatening remark? Where did your fiery little spirit go?" he questioned, trying to goad her. "What does the young Snowden prince see in you?"

Renya held her tongue. She didn't want to give him any information. She already worked out some of the answers she wanted. He called her human, which meant he didn't know about her heritage. He kidnapped her, hoping to get to Grayden. But why take her and not him? They must want something else from him, something they couldn't take without convincing him to give it up. What could that be? His lands? The little bit of magic he had left? It hit her. The marriage alliance. They were going to use her to force Grayden into marrying the Shadow Queen.

"Well, human," he pronounced the word as if it was an abomination, "I'm bored with you now. Oh–I hope you enjoy our accommodations. Just don't fall asleep. They call it the nightmare dungeon, and I'm sure you don't want to find out why."

Chapter Twenty-Seven

I t was dark when Grayden regained consciousness. He could hear a voice calling for him...Jurel, he thought. His head swam, but he could only think of one thing: Renya. He had to find her and get her back. But Fates, he felt weak and drained. He pushed all the magic he had into the wall protecting Renya. Reserves of magic he didn't know he possessed. But Brandle still managed to take her.

He sat up and saw a light ahead. Grayden looked around for Lightning, but didn't see him anywhere. He picked himself up and ran towards the source of the light at a sluggish pace, putting everything he had into getting to his lodge, finding a horse and tracking down Renya. However, it was an effort to put one foot in front of the other, but he wouldn't give up.

"Grayden!" a voice called out. "Renya! Are you out here?"

Grayden continued towards the light and voice. "Renya!" he shouted out. "Brandle took Renya!"

Jurel came into view on horseback, riding towards Grayden, Lightning trailing behind. "Grayden, what happened? Lightning returned to the lodge without you, and there's no sign of Frost."

Grayden was frantic. "Brandle came. He said he was looking for Selenia, but he saw Renya and I...he saw us together and took her instead."

At the mention of Selenia's name, Jurel's brow furrowed angrily.

"Quick, we have to head back to the lodge. We have to find her and get her back!"

"Do you have any plausible idea where he would have taken her?"

Grayden rubbed his temples. Where would Brandle take her? To the Shadow Realm? No, that would be too far for his magic to transport them. What was near? Somewhere Brandle could hold Renya prisoner. He needed a map.

"I'm not sure, but I'd say he wouldn't be able to travel over twenty-five miles by magic, thirty at most. He threw up some pretty heavy spells to keep me unconscious for so long, and he had to transport Renya, too."

Renya. Brandle had Renya. Was he hurting her? Was she scared? He hoped for her sake, wherever she was, she would still be unconscious from the magic used to transport her. He didn't want her cold and alone in some dungeon—it hit him.

"It's the Sunset Land, I'm sure of it. It's the closest thing nearby, and it's a fortress. Plus, their dungeons are enforced by magic." He didn't think he could feel any worse than he did now, but knowing where she was painted an even more vivid picture of her lying in the dungeon, shivering and cold.

Grayden moved towards Lightning and leaped up on the horse and took off as fast as he could, Jurel behind him. Even though he was pushing Lightning at top speed, everything seemed to go in slow motion and he felt like every second lasted an hour. The path back to the lodge never seemed to end.

He reached the courtyard and noticed countless horses. Phillippe must be back! Grayden hoped he could fight and was relieved some of their men had returned. He would need a full army to storm the Sunset Land Castle and rescue Renya.

Just as he was dismounting, he overheard one of the men talking to another.

"...we found her out in the snow. She must have come through a portal. The prince had found a portal earlier, but we don't know if it's the same one or not. I think they took her to Tumwalt."

Could they have found Renya? Was it possible she managed to get away through a portal and come back? Grayden's heart squeezed as he ran into the cabinet room where he met with his advisors.

He burst through the doors, nearly knocking them off their hinges. "Renya!" he bellowed.

Tumwalt, Phillippe, and Charly all stood around a table, looking at a large map of the area. They looked up at Grayden's outburst. Grayden scanned the room and saw a fourth person, but it wasn't Renya. It was an elderly woman. She glared at him and Grayden felt the hostility rolling off of her in waves. She looked straight into his eyes as she spoke.

"Are you going to explain to me how you managed to lose my niece, Boy?"

Chapter Twenty-Eight

G rayden looked the older woman up and down. She was wearing multiple layers of clothing and had a large carrying bag strapped against her back. Her face looked aged, but her voice sounded young and her eyes were bright. She had a large walking stick, which she brandished at Grayden with every word she spoke. Grayden felt the power radiating off of her and realized at once that she was Fae.

"Tell me, Boy, what have you done with her?"

Charly cleared his throat while the woman continued to glower at Grayden. "We came across this woman on our way back here. She asked if anyone had met a blonde-haired girl with blue eyes–"

"Renya," Grayden hissed.

"Yes, I told her about Mistress Renya, and she asked to come with us. Well, actually, demanded." He lowered his voice. "The old woman is quite powerful. She stopped the horses by magic alone."

The woman whacked Charly on the top of his head with her walking stick. "I'm not old, and my hearing is fine," she chided, as Charly rubbed the spot she hit.

"You're Renya's aunt? Agatha?" Grayden asked.

"Yes, I am, but more importantly, where is she? Your staff said you took her out riding, but here you are, without her. They found your horse, but not hers."

Grayden hung his head. "She's been taken." He

looked helplessly up at Phillippe, Charly, and Tumwalt. "It was Brandle. He saw us in the forest and took her as leverage. I think he's using Renya to get to me. To use her in the negotiations with the Shadow Queen."

Aunt Agatha looked at Grayden intensely, as if sizing him up. "Why would he think my Renya held any significance to you?"

Grayden was silent. A moment passed.

"Ah, I see. Well, I can't deny that I can see the appeal in your looks at least. The Snowdens were always a handsome lot. Tell me, Boy, does my niece return your feelings?"

Grayden didn't even try to deny the feelings he had for Renya. He felt them coming on the longer he spent with her but tried to shove them down, deep inside himself. However, once Brandle threatened her, they rose to the surface, and he knew he could no longer deny what he felt. "I don't know."

Phillippe, Charly and Tumwalt seemed uncomfortable.

"Well, you are going to help me get her back. I didn't spend my golden years in that Gods forsaken human realm and come all the way through that damn portal just to lose her. And to Brandle, of all people! He's an idiot! How is it possible he took her from you? He's a weakling."

"You know him?" Grayden asked, astonished.

"Unfortunately, I do. The greasy slimeball."

Grayden looked at her.

"It's a human barb. Their manners might be lacking, but their insults are top-notch," Agatha said.

"I don't know when you last saw him, but his powers have grown with the Shadow Queen's. Whereas mine have faded."

Agatha harrumphed. "So that part of the prophecy came true, then."

"You know about the prophecy?"

Agatha's fingers clutched around her stick like she wanted to hit Grayden with it, too. "Of course I do! Why do you think we sent her to the human realm with me? Seriously, I leave and apparently everyone left here is dumber than stumps..."

"Do you know the full prophecy?"

Agatha rolled her eyes and recited:

"When magic fades, light bringer returns
Power will flow and lust will burn
For balance to be restored, a sacrifice made
The shadows reveal and the sun betrays"

"A sacrifice made...I will not sacrifice Renya!" Grayden growled.

"Hold on to your pants, Boy. These things rarely make sense until after they come to pass. Prophecies..." she rolled her eyes. "They're worse than human weathermen...All we knew was Renya was most likely the light bringer, so we hid her in the human world. I tried my best to keep her away from any portal I could sense, but then she moved to Seattle, alone. I begged and pleaded, but you know how stubborn she can be."

Grayden nodded emphatically, but Agatha just glared at him. Apparently, she could say those things about her niece, but he couldn't.

"Renya described a situation that sounded like it could have potentially been an opening, and when she didn't return my calls, I came to Seattle to investigate. I found her empty apartment and went across the street and tracked her to the portal. I hoped to get here before it was too late, but apparently you couldn't hold off an imbecile like Brandle long enough for me to take her home."

Grayden accepted the insult. It was a low blow when he barely had any magic left, but he failed Renya after promising to keep her safe.

"Well, Boy, find me a horse. And a fast one, not some old retired mare. Saddle up, let's go get her back."

Grayden wanted to protest and leave Agatha behind, but it was clear that she possessed a great deal of magic and they would need everything at their disposal to get Renya back safely. He motioned to his men to get ready.

Within an hour, Grayden, Jurel, Charly and Agatha were riding hard towards the Sunset Land. Dimitri trailed behind. He couldn't keep up with the group, but he would follow behind and see to any injuries Renya might have. Grayden's stomach turned at the thought. He knew having Dimitri come along was practical, but the thought of Renya hurt made him feel physically ill and in need of the healer himself.

Phillippe had wanted to come as well, but Grayden was too concerned about his injury. He placed him in charge of watching over Selenia. He agreed, but Grayden could tell he was upset about not having Grayden's back.

Agatha, however, seemed to keep up with them just fine, despite her age. Grayden wondered if her age was some kind of disguise or if something had happened to her from spending so many years in the human realm.

"So what's your plan, Boy? Your father would have had a good one in mind," Agatha said.

"You knew my father?"

"Of course I did! Stop asking stupid questions and tell me what your plan is."

"It's me the Shadow Queen wants," Grayden said. "She seeks a marriage alliance. I'm going to accept her in exchange for Renya's freedom."

"Well, that's a dumb plan," she said. "And besides, she's too old for you."

"I'm aware," Grayden mumbled darkly, rolling his eyes.

"Well, that's not gonna work. She'll accept your proposal, but she won't let Renya go. Not when she finds out who she is. And she will find out as soon as she lays eyes on her, mark my words. Brandle might be too dense to realize it, but Cressida won't be."

"I'm open to suggestions."

"You said your magic is all gone, right, Boy?"

"Yes. I used my last reserves to try to save Renya," Grayden replied.

"Do any of your men have power?" she asked.

"They are all fine warriors who have proven their worth."

"A simple 'no' would have sufficed," Agatha said, rolling her eyes. "We'll need to use the element of surprise. Obviously, they know we'll be coming for her. But they don't know about me. I disappeared from this world over twenty years ago. Those possessing memories of me won't expect me to be alive. I do have magic, potent magic, but it's weakened a bit from being in the human realm. Luckily, it didn't fade like everyone else's, but it'll take some time to return to its full power. It won't be enough to take her on. The best thing we can hope for is a distraction so we can get Renya away long enough to send her home."

Grayden nodded. "Can you open the portal?"

"Yes," she responded. "I left a marker of my magic so I can open it to the right spot. But even without it, any human realm or time is better than her being here."

Grayden agreed. It was what was best for Renya. His heart sank at the thought of her returning to the human world, but it was the only way to keep her safe. "What kind of distraction are you thinking about?"

"Me," Agatha said. "Trust me, she won't be expecting me and she'll do anything to destroy me. If she does, you need to be prepared to send Renya back on your own. Like I said, time and place don't matter. She just can't be here. You need to find someone with magic, and fast to get that portal opened."

"I will," Grayden promised.

"Are you sure, Boy? I won't sacrifice myself if you can't give her up when the time comes."

Grayden's jaw clenched. "I will do whatever is best when it comes to Renya."

Agatha turned her head to study him, shifting the reins between her hands. Her gray hair was pulled back tightly and, despite her age, she looked formidable. "I believe you."

They rode hard for the rest of the day, only stopping minimally to water the horses. They approached a large spring when they crossed in the Sunset Land's boundaries, and everyone stopped to take a quick rest.

Grayden walked to the spring and cupped up some water and splashed it across his face. He stood up, stretching his legs and back. He was just getting ready to tell everyone that they needed to get going when a hawk cried out and circled the group. Grayden looked up and saw a message attached to the bird's foot.

"Sion!" he exclaimed, holding out his arm for the hawk to land.

The bird gracefully approached Grayden and perched on his forearm. He removed the parchment from the animal's foot quickly. Once freed from the message, the bird disappeared into the clouds.

Frantically, Grayden unrolled it and read:

G—

I know she's taken something from you. It's in the Sunset Land. I've subdued her powers. Use your time fast. The magic won't last long. Once she realizes what's happened, I'm sure she'll know it was me. If we don't see each other again in this world, I'll see you in the next.

—S

Agatha barely waited for Grayden to finish reading before she grabbed the letter out of his hands. "Who is Sion?" she demanded.

"I've had a spy within her court for six months now. He had gone silent, and I thought we lost him, but it sounds like he managed to do something to the Shadow Queen."

"Hmmm...maybe you're worth more than just your good looks. A spy, that's useful. Subdued her powers..." Agatha rubbed her fingers along her chin in thought. "It must have been a draft of some kind. Tell me, did he have direct access to her?"

Grayden cleared his throat uncomfortably. "He sent a letter two months ago saying he thought he might...seduce her. That was the last letter I got."

"Well, then it's definitely possible he managed to get her to take a draft. It's dangerous, especially given the timing of it. If it kicks in too soon, she won't be able to travel by magic and she'll realize it right away. Too late and we could all be dead. Still, whoever took this risk did us a huge favor. I might have been wrong about you, Boy."

Chapter Twenty-Nine

R enya pinched herself hard. Her body was so tired from the magic Brandle had used on her. But she was terrified of what he had said about nightmares. Was he lying? Did he just want to keep her on edge and wear her down?

Her eyes were so heavy. Suddenly, she heard a noise behind her and turned. Barely illuminated from the torch on the wall, a man in a crisp three-piece suit came towards her. His eyes glowed red and his hands were reaching for her. She screamed and scampered towards the other end of the cell, her back against the wet wall.

"Renya..." he purred, "you didn't think I'd help you without nothing in return, did you?" He crossed to her and reached out, stroking her cheek up and down with his sweaty palm.

Renya tried to push him away, but her hands were so heavy she couldn't lift her arms. She tried to get away from his grasp, but he had her backed into the corner of the cell.

"Besides, I know you want this too. You've been asking for it since the first day I met you," he sneered. "You're a talentless little tart, but you have a great ass."

Without warning, he pressed his lips against hers, hard. She fought frantically, screaming and kicking, but she couldn't get away from his cruel touch.

"Grayden!" she screamed. "Help me!"

Grayden appeared next to her. Renya felt relief for just a split second, until she noticed how pale he looked. His tunic was faded and gray, and his brown hair was practically silver.

"I can't help you, Renya," he said sadly. "My magic is gone and I'm dying." He held her gaze while the senator pressed his hand against her neck, holding her against the wall and strangling her.

She didn't know what she was more scared of: the senator holding her against the wall or Grayden next to her, dying. He was the one person who could save her and she needed him. She cared for him. She trusted him. It surprised her when she realized it, but she fully trusted him.

Grayden was slipping away fast. Tears rolled down her cheeks as she tried to reach out to him with her heavy hands. She needed to touch him, to say goodbye. To tell him how she felt about him. He lifted his hands to help her but was paralyzed by a dusky shadow, slowly circling around him.

The senator was morphing, his fingers growing into long claws, ragged against her skin. His face and body were contorting until he transformed into a tygre. She could feel his hot breath on her neck and the foamy saliva creep down her chest. Renya reached for a dagger, but she only had an umbrella. She tried to push the beast off of her with the umbrella, but it came closer and closer, snapping its jaws. She could smell the blood on its mouth.

"Grayden!" she screamed again. She turned her head, but he was already gone. She sobbed hysterically.

In his place was Aunt Agatha, holding a newborn baby. "It's okay, Renya. We'll just offer up this baby. It's part of a prophecy, so its life doesn't really matter."

Renya screamed as her aunt held up the baby to the frothing tygre.

The tygre in front of her disappeared, and this time, a dark green dragon took its place, filling up her entire cell. The dragon's bulk pushed her further against the wall with its scaly body. She realized she was against the magical barrier. It was no longer just a barrier, but an electric fence that shocked her every time she fell against it. The dragon brought its head down and sniffed at her before opening its mouth and letting loose a ball of white hot fire, talons swiping at her.

Renya screamed and screamed. She screamed until she had no voice and her throat was raw.

The next nightmare was even longer. The elements stayed the same, but left her physically weak when she woke. So weak that all she wanted to do was sleep. The cycle was unbearable, and she lost all sense of time. How long had she been here? A day? A week? She couldn't tell between the endless cycle of sleeping, screaming, waking, and sleeping again. The only thing allowing her to keep her sanity was the faint orange glow from the torch in the corner. She wrote stories in her head about it, epic fantasies that held her mind rooted in reality before the nightmares began again. The orange ball of light was the sun, and Renya was on a spacestation, millions of miles from Earth. Next it was the sunny horizon of a tropical beach. Renya held on to the stories tight, shielding her mind and strengthening her resolve. She would get out of here. She would survive. She would fight.

A voice called softly from the edge of the dungeon. At first, it was a gentle pull, easing Renya's consciousness back into the real world and tugging her away from the dragon, whose breath was scorching her clothes and burning her skin. The pull became stronger and stronger, and she could hear a single word through the dragon's roars.

"Selenia!" the voice called urgently. "Selenia! Are you here?"

Renya felt the cell shift and the dragon began to fade. Grayden's pale figure also faded, and she missed him when she woke. It was the only comforting thing in this prison. Sometimes she swore she could feel him with her, just tucked away somewhere safely inside.

"Selenia!" The voice came, more desperate but hardly above a whisper.

Renya forced her eyes open and looked around. She was on the dirty and damp floor of her cell, but alone. The dragon was gone. Her face was sore from being pressed against the cold stone, and her eyes were dry from all the crying. She was so thirsty. If she didn't stop crying, she was going to become dehydrated.

"Selenia!"

She heard it again and tried to lift her head, crawling towards the invisible barrier, her riding pants torn at the knees.

"Selenia, thank the Fates I found you! Your brother is on his way, I promise you–" the voice stopped as a man kneeled to look inside the cell.

Renya finally managed to lift her head. A tall, thin man squinted down at her. His bronzed skin and golden robes reflected off the light from the torch. His chocolate brown eyes landed on the elkten pin still fastened on her riding outfit. She grasped it in her hand at his inspection of it and the man's eyes immediately softened.

"Who are you?" he asked, confused.

"My name is Renya," she croaked, trying to stand up.

"Where is Selenia?" the man asked, searching over her shoulder like Selenia might be in the same cell.

"I don't know," Renya said faintly. "I was riding with Grayden and Brandle...he said he found me instead of Selenia." Renya pushed herself up against the wall, her shoulder aching from the pressure of holding herself up on her weak legs.

The man frowned. "All the planning I heard was that Selenia was supposed to be taken and used against Grayden. I tried to thwart it every step of the way, but when I couldn't, I attempted to get word to Grayden to warn him. The hawk I sent was shot down by one of her palace guards. I had to hunt the guard down so news of my betrayal wouldn't reach Queen Cressida's ears. I sent out another hawk, but I feared it would be too late."

Renya looked at him. "You're a spy."

"Yes, I am. Grayden sent me to the Shadow Realm to infiltrate her inner circle. I secured a coveted place in her court...and in her bed." He said the last part with absolute disgust.

"Can you help me?" Renya asked desperately, her hoarse voice straining in the near darkness.

"I'll do whatever I can," he replied. "I see you're wearing Grayden's elkten pin, so you're obviously someone he trusts. Although I must admit, I've never seen Grayden form any kind of attachment with a female..." he trailed off, looking at her with greater interest. "My name is Sion; I've known Grayden since we were boys together on the training fields in the mountains."

Renya slowly slid back down the wall, her strength

fleeting. Sion looked at her with sympathy in his warm eyes.

"Here, I had brought this for Selenia once I heard of their plan to keep her down here." He held out his hand and Renya saw a thin plant with an orange tint in his palm. He tried to pass it through the magical barrier, but he couldn't find an opening anywhere.

"Renya, I'm going to look for an opening in the barrier. I'm guessing that there is some place where the magic connects to the physical world and there might be a break there." Sion ran his hands along the bottom of the cell, and once he got to the corner, he was able to push the plant underneath. Slowly, centimeter by centimeter, the edge of the stalk slid under the invisible barrier.

Renya pulled it away from the edge of her cell and looked at it. "What is it?" she asked hoarsely, looking at the slimy tube in her hand.

"Tarot root. It will protect you from any outside magic for a little bit. It's incredibly rare, and I could only grab one stalk. I sneaked into her majesty's—sorry, old habits die hard," he said, correcting himself. "I managed to take this from the Shadow Queen's personal stock. Hopefully she will just think she miscounted. That bit might last anywhere from thirty minutes to two hours. It'll protect you for a little while from the nightmares. Don't eat it until you feel that you absolutely can't stay awake. Like I said, I think I got a message to Grayden on my way here, so he knows where you're at and he should be on his way. But I don't know how far out he is. I've done all I can to help without being exposed."

Renya looked into his sympathetic eyes. "Thank you," she said weakly.

Sion nodded. "You must be important to Grayden

if Brandle took you instead of Selenia. I hope to get a chance to meet you under better circumstances one day, Renya."

Chapter Thirty

They reached the Sunset Land Castle slightly before nightfall, or at least Grayden thought it was nightfall. Just like his lands were always covered in snow, this realm perpetually hovered between day and night. An orange glow bathed the land, but the shadows just on the edge turned everything into a sharp harshness. It made sense to Grayden that this would be where they would have taken Renya. It was one step away from the Shadow Lands.

Right in front of the castle stood a dark forest. The trees had no leaves, and the dark branches reached up like skeletons from a grave. It was eerily quiet, as if a single noise would break the balance between day and night in which the land permanently hung.

Grayden made his way carefully through the forest, his senses on high alert as he wove Lightning in and out of the dying trees. When the forest got thicker and darker, he motioned for the group to leave the horses.

"We'll continue the rest of the way on foot," he said, tying Lightning's reins to a tree. "When Dimitri catches up, he'll see the horses and know to wait for us here."

Charly and Jurel nodded, but Agatha spoke up. "Are we all going to enter at once and show our hand, or do we want to try for some element of surprise?" she asked.

"I think I need to go in first," Grayden said. "Queen

Cressida knows that I'll want to solve this with the least amount of violence as possible. I'm sure she's hoping I will agree to a trade and then she'll release her hostage and take me back to the Shadow Realm as both her fiancée and prisoner."

"She won't release Renya," Agatha reminded Grayden. "I'm going to have to come in and attempt to persuade her." Her fingers danced slightly with power and dark furrows crept slowly out of the tips before fading. It was clear to Grayden that she possessed significant magic.

Grayden nodded. "I'll go first, and appeal to the queen. When she thinks I've accepted the terms of a marriage alliance, I'll need you all to come in as back-up. The first priority is Renya. Once she's safe, our goal is accomplished and you leave. No matter what. Do you understand?"

Agatha agreed easily, but Charly and Jurel protested. "My lord, there is no way we will leave without you—" Charly began.

"I mean it, as your lord and prince, Renya is to be your first priority. She lives. She makes it home. That's an order."

Charly and Jurel exchanged a look but didn't argue with Grayden.

They made their way to the edge of the forest and up to a collapsing stone staircase leading to the castle.

"Should we all look for a back way in?" Jurel suggested.

"No," Grayden said, "we part ways here. I'm going to walk up the steps just like they expect me to. I want you three to find another way in and keep to the shadows. Don't show yourselves until we have eyes on Renya."

Jurel and Charly looked around awkwardly, trying to decide if they wanted to say goodbye just in case one of them didn't make it, but Grayden just slapped each man heartily on the back.

"Thank you both," he said sincerely. He bowed his head slightly to Agatha and then started up the crumbling steps while the rest of their party slinked back into the shadows.

The Sunset Land Castle was formidable looking. Meant to withstand sieges, it was impenetrable when fully guarded. Dark spires twisted up towards the blood red sky, and stone ravens were carved into the sides of the towers. Grayden heard a shrill call and turned his head toward one of the lower towers. A live raven was perched among the busts of them, watching Grayden's every move, his red eyes following.

Grayden kept climbing the crumbling stairs, finally reaching the portcullis. It was wide open, just as he suspected. He was walking right into their hands, like they suspected. Grayden just hoped that Renya's aunt would be enough to buy them time and get Renya out of there. He no longer cared about what happened to himself. Phillippe and Selenia would have Tumwalt to guide them. He only cared that Renya made it home alive.

He entered the castle, carefully stepping over fallen rubble. It was dark everywhere, except for a light ahead in what looked like a throne room. Grayden knew that was where he was supposed to go. Looking forward, he noticed that the ceiling of the great hall was gone. Instead, flocks of ravens sat everywhere. They all watched him, and the sensation made him nervous. He approached the throne room and saw more rubble everywhere. When the Sunset Land fell, no one was left to tell the tale. He wondered what happened here and what forces brought these parts of the castle down.

"Why if it isn't the love sick prince!" Brandle taunted from the back of the room. He was sitting sideways in a black throne made of obsidian, his ebony boots hanging off of one side. He was lazily smirking at Grayden as he approached.

"Funny," Grayden said, "I was wondering where your love sick queen was. I'm guessing that's the reason she's instructed you to take what's mine. She wants a marriage alliance."

"Bravo! That is exactly what she desires," Brandle said, clapping slowly. Grayden turned as several ravens took off to the sky at the sudden noise.

The only source of light in the room were four iron torches burning in each corner. Grayden glanced quickly around the room, sizing up any areas that attacks could come from. Where was the Shadow Queen? Was Brandle a distraction? His heart pounded. Did she already have Renya?

"Cut the games, Brandle. Where is Renya?" Grayden growled.

"Oh...she's fine. She's just sleeping off the aftereffects of our brief journey...in the nightmare dungeon."

Grayden turned pale. He had forgotten about the legends of the Sunset Land and their dungeons. He needed to get Renya, and fast. Grayden didn't want to leave her trapped there for another second. He'd heard tales of people going insane in the Sunset Land dungeons. His father once told them of a man that gouged out his own eyes after spending a night there. He was terrified for Renya.

"I'm here to make the deal," Grayden said. "Where is your evil bitch of a queen?"

"Tsk tsk," Brandle said, "that's no way to talk about your future bride. As it were, she should be here any minute. She wanted to make herself...exceptionally lovely for you."

Grayden snorted. But in his mind, he started calculating the draft Sion had given the queen. Was she not here yet because it had already taken effect and she couldn't travel? Or was she just trying to make an entrance? Or worst of all, had the effects already passed and they would all be up against her full power? He was expecting her to be here already.

"If you want to make any kind of treaty, you'll bring Renya here immediately," Grayden threatened. He caught movement out of the shadows as two men in golden robes came forward to join Brandle.

"As you can see, my dear prince, I don't think you are in any position to make demands."

Grayden hid his surprise as he looked at the men. The one on Brandle's left was Sion.

"You think that scares me, Brandle?"

"I'd hoped it would," Brandle said, pretending to be upset. "But look, here comes my queen now."

A dark, spinning funnel appeared in the middle of the throne room. It spun faster and faster, emitting tiny wisps of black smoke as it grew bigger and bigger. Grayden could just make out a dark, willowy silhouette through the dense cloud. His stomach turned, hating having to face her in person. With a spark of fire, the black smoke evaporated, and standing in front of Grayden was the Shadow Queen.

She turned her back to Grayden instantly, swaying

her hips and walking towards Brandle. With a flick of one long black nail, she motioned and Brandle got up out of the throne and stood to her right with the other man.

She sat down on the throne, crossing her legs, but making sure Grayden got a good look at her milky flesh. He felt like vomiting. Her blood red dress had a large slit in it, traveling all the way up her thigh. Her face was pale white and her lips were painted a bright red. She looked at Grayden with her purple eyes, her black hair shiny and straight.

"Why, my dear sweet prince," she cooed, her voice sickeningly sweet. "How wonderful of you to come and see me," she said, adjusting the pewter crown she wore on her head. "I was beginning to think you didn't care about me." She pretended to pout.

"I'm here for one reason. I've come for what's mine," he said through gritted teeth, ignoring the way Cressida stared at him like he was a meal. "Or else I wouldn't be here."

"Brandle sent word that he saw you with another girl. It hurt my feelings, my dear prince. We are, after all, going to be married."

"That remains to be seen." Grayden threatened, hoping she could see the malice he felt.

She pouted again, her red lips exaggerated. "Tell me, my sweet, handsome Grayden, is she prettier than me? Are her eyes as violet as mine? Are her lips as full as mine? Is her body as sultry as my body? Brandle said she's human. I can't imagine that she could hold a candle to my beauty." She pursed her lips and stood, careful to flash her thigh underneath the slit of her dress and twirled on her tall satin heels.

Grayden looked anywhere but at her. "She's more

beautiful than you could ever be, no matter how hard you try or however much power you steal."

Cressida stared at him, batting her lashes. "You wound me, dear prince," she said, turning towards Brandle. She dropped the saccharine tone she used with Grayden. "You better go get the disgusting human, and we'll see how she really measures up."

Grayden's heart leapt at the mention of Renya. Once she was brought in, they could take her and leave this place and he could get her home safely.

"In the meantime, let's have a little chat, you and me," she said, walking towards Grayden. "I'll make you a deal. You agree to the marriage alliance and crown me Queen of the Snow Lands, and your little human whore can go free." She trailed her sharp nail down the bit of Grayden's chest that was exposed under his shirt.

He flinched, repulsed by her touch. She smirked and leaned into him, whispering in his ear. "Don't you want a taste of my power? I'd give you a bit if you manage to please me." She cackled, clearly enjoying the game she was playing. She looked like a cat about to pounce.

"I will only consider marriage if you stick to our deal. You can have me, but she goes free, unharmed. I'll give you my word. But she is not to be touched or hurt."

Before she could respond, Brandle re-entered the throne room, pushing a frightened Renya towards the center of the room. Grayden could see instantly that she was incredibly weak. His heart ached at the sight of her. His brave, sweet Renya, broken in the nightmare dungeon. He tried to look for that fire she held in her eyes, but he could only see horror. She was still wearing the riding outfit from before, but she was missing the gloves. Her cloak was torn, but his heart rushed when he noticed she still had his little elkten symbol pinned near her throat. Renya's eyes were red from crying and her face was covered in scrapes, dirt, and tears. Her pretty blonde hair was ash colored from the dirt and grime of the dungeon, practically dulled to gray.

Grayden's heart soared to see her alive. Even as she was, she was the most alluring woman in the world to him.

The Shadow Queen sauntered over to Renya and gave her a shove towards Grayden. "See how clumsy and ungraceful she is?"

Weakened from her ordeal in the nightmare dungeon, Renya lost her footing and fell to her knees in front of Grayden. Sobbing in relief, she crawled towards him, trying to reach the protective circle of his strong arms. Before Grayden could pull her to him, Brandle grabbed her under the arms and yanked her back toward the throne. Renya kicked and screamed obscenities. She thrashed and managed to kick him hard in the groin. He fell backwards, cursing, and Grayden swore he saw the briefest grin cross Sion's face before it shifted back to neutrality.

"You dirty whore!" Brandle roared, raising his hand to strike Renya. Before he could land the blow, Grayden had crossed the floor and grabbed him by the neck. He lifted Brandle off the floor and squeezed. Brandle struggled for air, his face turning a dark maroon.

A titter came from the other side of the room. The Shadow Queen laughed and pulled Renya towards her sharply, her nails digging into Renya's shoulders. "Drop him, or your little harlot will never see the light of day again." Black smoke slithered from Cressida's fingers and started to close around Renya's throat, tightening.

Grayden released Brandle and pushed him hard into a column. "Let her go!" Grayden yelled. "I've given you my word. I'll marry you if you free her."

"No!" Renya screamed hoarsely. "Grayden, you can't!"

"Grayden, you can't!" the Shadow Queen mocked, trying to capture Renya's admonished tone. "I can do whatever I please and no one can stop me. Tell me, does this little tramp have a name?"

Cressida didn't even bother to look at Renya as she roughly pushed her again. This time, Grayden caught Renya and took her into his strong arms. She trembled and clutched at him, desperately seeking comfort.

"On second thought, I don't think I want to permanently attach myself to anyone who's had a human in their bed. Especially one so dirty...she even smells odd," Queen Cressida said, taking Renya in for the first time. "I'll just take your lands and find someone else to warm my bed. After all, I just need an heir—" she stopped talking and stared as Renya clung tightly to Grayden. Cressida's face turned even paler, as if she had seen a ghost.

Before Cressida could make another move, a blast of shadow hit her, throwing her against the glassy black throne.

Agatha stormed into the throne room, magic sizzling and crackling around her. Queen Cressida stood, taking in the scene before her. As soon as she saw Agatha, her mouth dropped wide.

"It's you!" she hissed at Agatha.

"Surprised? Your little death curse didn't work. None of the magic you weaved that night worked." Agatha glanced at Renya. Queen Cressida followed her gaze and another wave of shock passed through her.

Charly and Jurel burst into the room, swords raised. Brandle immediately raised a hand to let his magic flow, but Grayden threw himself at him, and Brandle missed and hit part of the collapsing ceiling. More rubble fell, nearly hitting Renya as she scurried away. She looked at her aunt, mouth wide open.

The other guard ran towards Grayden, trying to pull him off of Brandle. Sion ran over to Charly and Jurel.

"Sorry," Sion muttered as he punched Jurel in the jaw. "Make it look real," he encouraged Jurel quietly. Jurel suppressed a grin and threw a punch back at him. Sion fell to the ground and lay there, even though Jurel hardly touched him.

Charly and Jurel both made quick work of the other guard and joined Grayden in pinning Brandle.

"Stop messing with him and get the girl!" Queen Cressida yelled at Brandle. "I no longer care about Snowden! Grab the girl and go!" Cressida dodged another blast of magic from Agatha and crouched behind the throne. Grayden could see from his vantage point that the queen had no usable power. She was frantically trying to weave her magic and he could see panic on her face as her fingertips sparked, but nothing came forth. He silently thanked the Fates for Sion.

Brandle freed himself, and before they could stop him, his dark magic reached out to grab Renya. The black tendrils stopped right in front of her and then parted like the sea and passed her. He tried again with another jolt of power to no effect, and Cressida screamed in anger and fear.

"Go! Now!" Agatha screamed, focusing her magic on Brandle as he pivoted towards Grayden. Before he could unleash his power, Agatha pinned him to the floor.

Grayden scooped Renya up in his arms, running out of the collapsing castle with Charly and Jurel following. He heard another crack of magic behind him, and Cressida screamed again.

He flew down the steps as more rubble fell from the towers. He hoped Agatha was alive. Grayden needed her to open the portal to send Renya back. If she didn't make it out, he did not know where else to find someone with that kind of power so quickly. The game they played with the Shadow Queen wouldn't work a second time, and she would come after them, and soon.

Grayden landed at the bottom of the steps and took off for the forest, branches hitting his knees and face as he protected Renya against his chest. The ground underneath their feet trembled, and Grayden had a feeling that Agatha had gotten her full strength back.

They finally reached the horses and Grayden untied Lightning, lifting Renya up and swinging himself up behind her. For the first time since Renya was taken in the forest, Grayden felt relief as he pulled her tightly to him. She was alive. She was safe. And most surprising of all, she was still sane despite the time she spent in the dungeon.

"My aunt!" Renya squealed. "We can't leave her!"

"Renya, the plan was to save you no matter the cost, and that's what I'm doing."

She protested, but Jurel cut her off. "Look!" he said, pointing back towards the castle. They could see Agatha scurrying down the steps.

Charly took off on his horse towards her, and Grayden grabbed Lightning's reins as he gripped Renya even tighter.

Lightning galloped at top speed until they were out of the dark forest.

"What is this place?" Renya asked.

"The Sunset Land." Grayden answered, remembering that she traveled to the castle through magic.

Renya shuddered. "It's awful."

"Indeed, it is," Grayden explained. "It used to be beautiful, or so I was told. Everything was bathed in a romantic glow. But now, abandoned and dilapidated, it looks like a nightmare."

Renya shivered. "Please don't say the word nightmare to me for a very long time."

Grayden just kissed the top of her head and pressed Lightning on.

As they approached the outskirts of the Sunset Land, they saw Dimitri riding towards them. He noticed the speed at which they were traveling and turned his horse back the way he came, now leading the party back to the Snow Lands. Grayden and Renya caught up to him and Dimitri rode alongside the pair, looking them over carefully for injuries.

"Does anyone need immediate attention?" Dimitri asked.

"Renya needs to be looked over as soon as we can stop," Grayden commanded.

Dimitri nodded, and Grayden surged ahead on Lightning, continuing the grueling pace. He didn't allow anyone to stop until they crossed into the Snow Lands. He knew they were tired and exhausted, but since Brandle and Cressida could both travel by magic, they needed to get as far away as they could.

The group approached a small stream, and

Grayden finally signaled for everyone to stop. Jurel groaned as he slid off his horse, stiff and tired.

Grayden dismounted and grabbed Renya by the waist and helped her down. She stood in the embrace of his arms, and he pulled her close and kissed her passionately. She leaned into the kiss, and he cupped her cheeks in both hands and then pressed his forehead against hers as their eyes met. He kissed her again and again until there was no confusion as to who Renya belonged to.

Renya sat on a log as Dimitri looked her over. Besides several surface cuts and a few bruises, she was fine. Grayden made Dimitri look her over twice before he was satisfied. Grayden sat next to her on the log and held her hand in his the entire time the healer examined her. He could tell Dimitri was annoyed, but he didn't care. He was going to hold on to her as long as he could until he had to send her back.

"Jurel, I want you to head back and see if Charly and Agatha are behind us," Grayden said, still refusing to let go of Renya. "Dimitri, you go with him in case she's injured."

Jurel nodded and took off, Dimitri trailing behind him.

Grayden finally let go of Renya and reached into the bag Dimitri left, pulling out a piece of clean cloth. He went to the stream and wet it and came back and sat next to Renya.

He warmed up the cloth in his hands and gently began cleaning Renya's face. He wiped away the tears and dirt until her face was pink and clean. She was quiet and said nothing to him while he tended to her. He washed the cloth off in the stream and started on her hands next.

Only when she was clean, the traces of the dungeon off of her skin, did he finally break the silence.

"Renya, I'm so sorry. I never meant for you to get hurt. I shouldn't have let my guard down. Believe me, I wish I would have figured out a way to send you back the second I found you in the woods."

Renya just looked at him, her eyes dull.

"Are you doing okay? I know Dimitri said you were okay physically, but Brandle said they had you in the nightmare dungeon."

At his question, her lip quivered. He pulled her tight, crushing her against him.

"Oh Grayden, it was awful. My worst fears, everything I fear will happen, kept happening over and over on a loop. The senator attacked me, you kept fading away, and then there were tygres and a dragon—"

"Hush, my sweet one. You're safe now." At some point, her braid had come undone. He grabbed a section of her hair and began combing through it with his fingers, working the tangles out the best he could.

"I thought it would break me, but it didn't. I wrote stories in my mind and kept myself sane. Oh, and Grayden! Sion came! He gave me some kind of root that helped keep the dreams away."

Grayden sighed. "It seems like I owe a lot to Sion this evening," he said. "The root must have been what kept Brandle's powers from touching you. Sion also muted the Shadow Queen's magic, although I think your aunt would have been fine, regardless."

Renya looked up at him as he combed through another section of her hair, undoing a knot that formed along her temple. "I can't believe that all this time, my aunt was Fae. And her magic! Did you see it?"

"It would have been hard to miss," he replied.

"I guess there's no doubt that I'm this light bringer," she whispered.

"It doesn't matter anymore. You're going home."

"What?" Renya said, the surprise evident in her voice.

"Your aunt marked the portal she came through and as soon as we get there, you're both returning to the human realm. It's the only way to keep you safe and out of the Shadow Queen's clutches. I think she discovered you are part of the prophecy."

Before Renya could reply, they heard hoofbeats pounding and saw Agatha, Jurel, Charly and Dimitri riding towards them.

"Auntie!" Renya screamed, and stood up weakly.

"Oh, my dear!" Aunt Agatha exclaimed, dismounting with far too much ease for someone her age. She rushed over to Renya and pulled her into her arms. "Let me look at you! Are you okay?"

"I'm fine," Renya said, as her aunt held her at arm's length, examining her.

"What happened back there?" Grayden asked Agatha, looking behind her almost as if he expected Cressida to be following. "Were you able to destroy her?" He looked at her hopefully. If the threat was gone, he could keep Renya here with him.

Agatha shook her head no. Grayden frowned. Her magic was incredibly strong and against a powerless Cressida, she could have easily finished the job. He waited for an explanation, but none came. He wanted to discuss it further, but Renya spoke.

"I think we have some things to talk about," she said, looking at her aunt with love but also with a shadow of disappointment and betrayal.

Agatha's face fell as if she knew this was coming. "I think you're right, Sunshine. Let's rest my horse and then you can ride with me for a while and we'll talk."

Grayden flexed his fists and tried to remind himself that Renya wasn't his. She was going home. As much as he wanted her in his arms and on his horse, she needed this time to talk with her aunt and to figure out who she was, and there was no one better than Agatha for the job. He settled for riding back and forth, guarding them from the side.

Renya rode with her aunt until it came time for the group to separate. Jurel, Dimitri and Charly planned to head back to the lodge to strengthen their holdings and to figure out a way to guard their lands, and Renya, Agatha, and Grayden were going to head towards the southern borders to the portal.

Renya dismounted the horse she and Agatha rode on, and so did Charly and Jurel. She gave each man a hug.

"Thank you for coming to rescue me," she said. "Please take care of Grayden for me," she whispered.

Jurel looked embarrassed, but Charly gave Renya a bow of his head.

"I wish I could come back with you and say goodbye to Selenia," she said, disappointment clear in her blue eyes.

Agatha shook her head no. "I'm sorry, Sunshine, but to be honest, I'm surprised Cressida hasn't tried to get to us yet. She must be back at the Shadow Realm, trying to figure out what happened to her powers. I'm afraid we don't have time to waste. Once she feels secure enough in her magic, she will seek you out."

"Why didn't you kill her?" Grayden asked. It would

have solved all his problems. He knew it wasn't her responsibility to do so, but surely, she should have taken the chance. Did she want to ensure Renya couldn't stay here with him? Grayden could tell she disliked him, but would she really try to keep them separated?

"I just can't. Let's leave it at that, Boy." Grayden didn't pressure her anymore. What was done, was done and the chance was gone.

They watched Jurel and Charly ride away, with Dimitri trailing after them. Once the trio disappeared through the snowy woods, Renya, Grayden and Agatha turned towards their horses. Grayden pulled Renya up on his lap, looking at Agatha as if to dare her to try to stop him. Renya settled easily into his arms as if it was where she always belonged, and Lightning began trotting.

"So what did your aunt tell you?" he asked her. "Do you feel like talking about it?"

"Actually, I do," she said, resting her head back against his shoulder. "I didn't think I would want to, but talking about it helps me process it. And you're the only person outside my aunt that will understand. Once I'm back in my world..." she bit her lip.

"You won't be able to talk to anyone else," he finished sadly.

"Yes. It was a lot to take in. And I'm angry that she didn't tell me who I really was. She could have prevented this entire experience if she would have just told me."

"What else did you learn?"

"So, I am a descendant of the Sun Realm. You were right about that. I'm the last descendant, if my aunt is right. After the kingdom fell, my parents went into hiding, I guess. Their seer told them what he suspected about me and the prophecy, so they sent me to the human realm with Aunt Agatha so no one could use me. Aunt Agatha said that my parents couldn't be the ones to take me to the human world without causing too much suspicion," she said thoughtfully. "I'm not sure what happened to them, though. I guess they still could be out there somewhere. Aunt Agatha said she wasn't sure. There's no easy way to communicate across the portals."

"So you are full Fae?" he asked. "Why don't you look pure Fae? Your ears are human."

"You don't like the way I look?" Renya teased, reaching up and stoking her own ears absentmindedly.

"I love the way you look, Renya." He lowered his voice so her aunt couldn't hear. "I'd love the look of you naked even more."

Renya blushed and turned more red than he had ever seen her, and he loved it. He pictured her beneath him, under his furs, and he took a deep breath, trying to calm himself and push the image out of his mind before he acted on it right there in the forest.

Once she recovered from his teasing, she continued telling him what she learned. "You were right in your suspicions before. My aunt said there's a permanent glamor on me to hide any Fae features."

"I wonder if that's the magic Selenia sensed," Grayden pondered. "I have seen no signs of magic come from you. If you had powers, we should have known by now."

Renya pushed a piece of hair out of her face. "It's probably the glamor you and her sensed," she said. "There's just so much that I don't know."

"You'll have lots of questions and your aunt will answer them as soon as you're back in your world," he said confidently, looking at the elderly woman riding a little ways in front of them.

"I guess…" she said. "I still feel like myself, even though I'm supposed to be important to this prophecy thing. Aren't I supposed to be all powerful or something?"

Grayden rubbed his chin thoughtfully. "Sometimes it's the biggest things that make the smallest difference, and sometimes it's the smallest things that make the biggest difference. We don't know which one you might be."

"That's a good way to look at," she said, leaning back into him.

Chapter Thirty-One

A lthough she was incredibly tired, Renya enjoyed resting against Grayden, being surrounded by his warmth. She wished fervently that she didn't have to leave him. Now that her aunt was here, the human realm didn't hold her there like it did before. She could imagine a life with him here. She assumed that they would all work together to defeat the Shadow Queen. How could he send her back? What about his people? His lands? Their budding relationship?

Renya caught Aunt Agatha watching them carefully, a slight frown on her weathered face. Renya wondered if she didn't approve of Grayden, or if she just didn't want her forming ties here. But like it or not, there were things about this world—the world she was born into—she would be sad to leave behind. She would miss Selenia's loving insults towards her brother. She wouldn't get to see Selenia get married or intercede on Jurel's behalf when Grayden got too protective. Renya wouldn't get to know Phillippe. She wouldn't meet Starlia's foal. She never said goodbye to Doria, she realized. And the clips. Her heart dropped. The gorgeous snowflake clips Grayden gifted her lay on the side table next to her bed. Wait, not her bed. The bed in Grayden's guest room. That's what it would go back to. Just an empty room in his lodge. She wondered how fast he would move on. Would he find someone else? Her heart lurched at the thought and a wave of sheer panic went through her as she thought of Grayden with another woman. But she couldn't think that way. Once she stepped through the portal, she wouldn't have any claim to him or his future.

Her heart raced fast with the panic of it all, and she knew Grayden could sense her distress and felt his aching need to comfort her.

"It's getting dark," he said, surveying the skyline. "I think we should make camp."

"I agree," Agatha said. "It'll be easier to find the portal and travel through it in daylight, too."

They didn't have a tent, but Grayden found a spot on a hill and was able to work with the natural slope of the land and build a small snow shelter to protect them from the wind.

Agatha built a fire away from the shelter and took up camp there.

"You and Renya can sleep in the cave. I'll sleep on the ground," Grayden said, putting some final touches on the snow cave.

Agatha looked at the snow shelter and then back at the roaring fire. "I think I'll take my chances near the fire," she said.

Grayden went to the side packs that Lightning was carrying and pulled out some supplies to make tea. He watched the snow melt in the pot, his eyes unblinking and his mind a million miles away. He offered each of them a cup. Renya sat next to him, tucked into his arm with his warm fur cape covering both of them.

Renya looked up at Grayden, sorrow in her voice. "I left the snowflake hair clips at the lodge."

"Oh Renya," he said, cupping her face in both

hands and kissing her cheeks tenderly. His hands released her and played with his elkten pin on her cloak. He unpinned it and curled it into her fingers. "You'll always have this to remember me by."

She looked at it between her fingers and rubbed the silver, feeling the embossed design. Renya felt her eyes moisten. She'd never give up the little silver elkten. She'd wear it every day.

Agatha suddenly shifted away from them and spread the sleeping bag she brought with her in front of the fire. She turned her head and seemed to fall asleep. Renya wasn't sure if she was trying to give them privacy or if it disappointed her that Renya had fallen for Grayden so quickly. Renya never had a serious boyfriend before, and her aunt had never seen her even hug a man. She'd had some relationships in college, but they were far away from her aunt's prying eyes.

With Renya's aunt settled in and sleeping–or at least feigning sleep–Grayden kissed Renya, slow and determined, and she quietly moaned into his mouth. He pulled away too fast and stood. "Let's get you to the snow shelter," he said, pulling her to her feet. He held her by the arm and guided her to the sloped hill and the white little cave.

"How did you know how to make this?" she asked him.

"I've been making them since I was young," he answered. "With the furs, you should be plenty warm."

She frowned as they approached the small little entrance. "You won't stay with me?"

"No, I was planning to sleep in front of the fire and let you and your aunt sleep here. She obviously had other plans." His eyes glanced back to the fire, where Renya's aunt lay.

Renya looked into his eyes and raised her hand to push the mess of soft curls out of his face. She was going to miss his unruly hair.

"Grayden, stay with me," she pleaded. "I need you. I'm...afraid to go to sleep by myself after what happened in the dungeon. Please, I need to sleep with your arms wrapped around me."

Renya could tell the second his resolve faded. She was glad for it. She was independent and never needed a man before, but it was different with Grayden. He rebuilt her. She trusted him. Her vulnerability around him didn't make her feel weak, but gave her strength because she chose it. Renya couldn't believe it, but the horrors from her past were being slowly erased by every soft touch, longing glance, and lingering kiss. Renya had this man to thank for it. As mad as she was at her aunt for concealing her identity, if she hadn't fallen through the portal, she would have never met Grayden.

He motioned for her to crawl in the snow cave, and she shimmed in on her knees, him following behind her. Together they nestled beside each other in the privacy of the snowy den.

Chapter Thirty-Two

Grayden couldn't believe he was going to lose her. But he knew. He knew the horrors awaiting Renya if she stayed. Queen Cressida wouldn't stop until she got her back. Killed her. And Grayden couldn't live with himself. She was too valuable. Too precious. He loved her too much.

Ah, yes. Love. He loved her. How long had he loved her for? Longer than he realized. He and Renya may not be fate-bonded, but he knew what he felt for her was real. How else could he give her back to the human world? He had been telling himself he protected her and took care of her for the good of the realm and for the importance she held for the prophecy, but he could no longer lie to himself. He loved her and her alone.

His heart tightened as he thought about what tomorrow would bring. He didn't know how he would say goodbye or if he would survive it. He almost wished Brandle had killed him. It would have been far less painful than sending Renya back through the portal.

Outside of the cave, Renya's aunt snored in her sleep. By this time tomorrow, Renya would be back in her own world with her. His chest constricted painfully at the thought.

Grayden looked down at Renya, her eyes staring into the side of the snow cave vacantly. She rested warmly on a bed of his furs, her back to his chest. Did she feel it too? Did she love him?

He placed a hand on her shoulder, and she turned her head to look at him. Grayden gently kissed her forehead, his lips slightly parted. He pulled back and looked into her eyes. Tears clung to her lashes, freezing in place. Grayden brought his mouth down and gently kissed her eyelids, his tongue darting out to caress her lashes slowly and melt the frozen tears. A shudder moved down her body and she gasped his name softly. Reverently.

"Grayden..."

His resolve was quickly disappearing. He might not be able to keep her, but for tonight, he wanted her. Given her insistence that he join her in the shelter, he knew she needed him too. Grayden wanted to etch her memory into his soul. She would never be his and he would never have a future with her, but at least he could show her how he felt. He didn't dare speak of his love. He had no right to her. But for tonight, he could be hers, even if fate deemed she would never be his.

He gently pressed a finger to her lips, signaling that whatever was about to transpire between them in this moment had to happen quietly. He felt her warm exhale against his finger and he sighed. Grayden removed her cloak, pushing her hair away from her neck, and slowly began kissing her. Renya's mouth opened and closed as he continued down to her collarbone, suckling and marking her with his mouth. It wasn't a mating mark, but for the next few days she would bear witness to his passion, even if she would never officially be claimed by him.

Renya writhed under his touch, her eyes wide and

her mouth moving wordlessly. He stopped his assault against her neck long enough to bring two of his fingers up to her lips.

"Open," he whispered hotly into her ear.

She obeyed and took his fingers inside her mouth. He trembled as he imagined what her mouth would feel like on his member. She swirled her tongue against his fingers, and he felt himself harden and press against her back. She tried to reach behind her and grab him, but he gently pushed her hands down. Tonight was about her.

He pulled his fingers from her mouth and made his way down her beautiful legs. He parted her riding skirt and moved underneath the leather trousers, slowly working his way downward as she moaned.

"Hush now, little one," he purred. "I've got you."

Grayden continued his trail down to her warm center. His other hand reached to the front of her dress and undid the laces before reaching a hand inside and freeing her breasts. Renya gasped as the coldness hit her nipples, but at the same moment, Grayden grazed his fingers along the apex of her thighs. She shivered, and he began kissing her earlobe while his fingers teased her.

He pressed his palm against her sensitive spot and began tracing the crease of her breasts and her hard nipples with his other hand.

Gods, he didn't know how he would give her up.

She moved her hips, trying to urge him on, to set a faster pace, but he only blew warm air gently against her ear.

"Oh, Little Fawn, so impatient, aren't you?" Taking pity on her, he moved his fingers, coated in her saliva, to her entrance. Her eyes widened and she gasped as he pushed his finger inside her, checking for wetness. When he felt the moisture pooled inside, he added another finger. Fates, she was tight! Were all human women this small inside?

"Is this okay?" he whispered, his eyes searching hers.

She nodded yes and then quivered, her body taut and her eyes closed. Grayden bit his lip as he felt his member twitch. Gods, if he wasn't careful, he was going to come just from watching her pleasure.

She moved with him, thrusting her hips desperately to meet his hand. He rested his forehead against hers, then curled his fingers inside her while his palm circled the bundle of nerves at the apex of her sex. He found the sensitive spot inside her and pressed lightly as she arched her back against him and her legs started to shake.

"That's my girl. Let me send you home with a happy memory of our time together," he coaxed, rubbing small circles inside her. He pulled his two fingers out completely, and she whimpered. He gave them back to her quickly, stroking and rubbing her inner walls as they clenched with her impending release. Grayden could feel her muscles trying to pull his fingers deeper inside her throbbing sex. He inserted another finger, stretching her even further, and then licked the small red mark he had made on her neck. "Never forget me, Renya," he pleaded, the desperation in his voice thick.

Her body convulsed as she fell apart in his arms. The second she reached her release, he felt his member lengthen and harden even more. He planned to hold back, but watching her face contorted in pleasure sent him nearly over the edge. He thought of all the times he put his kingdom, his family, and duty first. Everything else before his needs. He also knew he'd never want another woman the way he wanted Renya.

With a moan, he withdrew his fingers from her body and quickly unlaced his trousers to pull out his rigid member. He pumped himself once, twice and then rolled over and released hot mounds of his seed into the snow. He groaned softly with each contraction of his member as the waves of pleasure rolled over him and more and more seed joined the pile. His pleasure seemed to last forever. Grayden couldn't remember ever coming with such force or intensity, and he wasn't even within her. What would it be like to be surrounded by her? He pushed the dream away as he pulled her toward him with one arm. He lay there, satisfied in a way he hadn't been in years. Perhaps ever.

Renya trembled with little aftershocks and looked into Grayden's eyes, tears threatening to fall again from her thick lashes. He pushed a few loose strands of hair back from her forehead and kissed her, slowly pulling her bottom lip into his mouth. Grayden watched her eyes darken primitively as brought his fingers to his mouth and licked her moisture off them. He tasted the saltiness from her arousal, but there was also something else. Copper? Iron?

Blood. There was a slight tinge of blood mixed in with her desire.

He cupped her face with both hands, frantically looking for signs of residual pain in her face. "My love, did I hurt you?"

She lowered her lashes and sighed. "No, I'm okay."

"No, I must have hurt you, you were so small and tight and I—"

Realization dawned on him. The slight resistance

he felt when his third finger entered her. No. Fates, no!

"Renya, was this…Did I…had you—" he trailed off.

A rush of pink crept up her neck. Of all things to be embarrassed about, especially given the fact that he just had his fingers inside her and the taste of her on his tongue. "It's no big deal," she whispered.

Grayden shook with anger at himself. It shouldn't have been like this, stolen moments on his furs, her slumbering aunt thirty feet away. Renya deserved a bed of lotus petals, satin and silk beneath her, with heat and warmth and tenderness. With her true fated mate. Not the sad desperation in which he'd pleasured her.

He thought the senator—what had she said? He attacked her? She was vague. Did he actually not fully take her? He must not have. Relief at the thought spread through him, followed by his own shame.

Gods. How could he have done this? She would never belong to him; he took something that wasn't his. Grayden's arousal was long gone, water thrown onto the fire of his lust. He was selfish and weak, and now he felt tortured by it.

"Hey," she said tenderly, kissing his jaw and feeling the coarse stubble on her lips as if she sensed his inner turmoil. "I wanted it to be with you. I—I needed it to be you. You've put me back together, Grayden. I was broken and you've made me whole again."

Grayden hadn't shed a single tear since entering manhood. Not even as his parents' coffins were lowered into the ground. Not in frustration as he watched his kingdom and his magic falter. Not when the tygres attacked him or when Renya stitched him up. He knew life was full of pain, but weakness and tears had no place in a ruler. Grayden was strong. He seized situations and took control. But looking at Renya's trembling lips, her hands desperately clutching his body tightly to hers, broke him.

He turned his head away, tears freezing in the corner of his eyes, and wrapped his arms around his beloved.

Chapter Thirty-Three

Daylight came quickly, and Grayden and Renya packed up the camp silently. Grayden said nothing else to her for the rest of the night. There was nothing to say. He just held her, breathing warmly against the back of her neck. She didn't think either of them slept. The loss was too great for both of them. Yet there was no choice. Renya knew what staying in this world meant. It would be a death sentence for her. It was ironic; she hadn't wanted to stay until the choice was made for her. She could now admit to herself that she wanted to remain here with Grayden. Wanted to be with him. Renya wanted to eat breakfast with him every morning and ride with him during the day. She wanted to crawl into his bed every night and make love. Renya wanted to shop with Selenia and gossip about Jurel. She sniffed, holding back tears.

Grayden heard her and came over. He gently put his arm around her and pulled her to his chest. They stood like that for a long time until Aunt Agatha gently told them it was time to go.

Grayden pulled Renya on top of his horse for the last time, and she leaned into him, not bothering to hide her tears.

It seemed to take no time at all to reach the clearing where she had first entered his world. He dismounted and lifted Renya down. Aunt Agatha opened the portal and then studied it, making sure everything seemed in order.

"I'm going to go through first, Renya. That will give you time to say goodbye," Aunt Agatha said, stepping towards the shiny archway she had brought forward in the middle of the forest. She walked towards it, and with a gust of wind, she was gone.

Renya started sobbing. "I can't go," she cried. "I want to stay here with you."

Grayden rested his forehead on hers, and she closed her eyes, memorizing the sensation of his skin against hers. "You have to go, my Little Fawn. I would give anything to keep you here, but it's not safe for you. Once you go through, your aunt will permanently close the portal. Queen Cressida won't be able to come after you. You'll be safe."

"What good is being safe if I'm miserable?" she asked, the tears flowing freely down her cheeks. Grayden choked back a sob and kissed her jawline.

"I need you to be safe, Renya. If you stayed because of me and something happened to you here, I could never live with myself. I want you to live a long and happy life. Even though it's not going to be with me."

Renya could hardly breathe. Every single part of her body hurt. How could this be goodbye? She wasn't ready. She didn't get enough time with him. No matter how long she had, it would never be enough.

Grayden tucked a stray piece of hair behind her ear and tenderly brought his mouth to hers. She cried as she kissed him, and she knew he could taste the saltiness of her tears. She tried to put everything she felt into that one last kiss.

He broke away too soon, and Renya trembled as she looked up at him. He looked absolutely shattered.

"It's time," he said, kissing her on the forehead like he had done so many times before. "Any longer and it's just going to be more painful than it already is."

Renya nodded, and he clenched her hand as she approached the portal. She leaned forward, and she felt Grayden tightened his hand around hers. He held onto her fingers until the very end, when the large blast of wind pulled her from him and she disappeared from their world.

Chapter Thirty-Three

R enya's head pounded as she collapsed onto the basement floor of The Rainy-Day Bookstore. Her whole body felt like it was on fire. She breathed a few deep breaths and kept her eyes closed. She still felt the tears, wet on her cheeks, running down onto the floor. Renya could still smell Grayden on her, his warm pine and spice smell. Every single part of her hurt, from her body to her mind to her soul. The first time she traveled through the portal, it was just physical pain. This time, her heart was broken and she didn't think she could breathe as she lay there, defeated by circumstance.

"Renya!" Aunt Agatha screamed.

Renya quickly looked up, confused. What was going on? Her eyes darted around the long hall until she saw her aunt.

Aunt Agatha was paralyzed in the far corner, a dark cloud holding her in place.

Renya screamed as a shadow fell on her aunt, signaling someone coming down the basement stairs. She watched her aunt writhing helplessly and ran towards her.

"Did you really think I'd let you go?" Queen Cressida said in her sultry voice, her high-heeled shoe hitting the last step. "We're going to get to know each other so well, Renya."

Cressida grabbed her tightly, and Renya tried to

fight before she was bound once again by magic. In an instant, she was being pushed through a different door. She barely had time to take in the small seashell carved into the door before darkness claimed her and she fell.

Renya and Grayden's story continues in part two of the Sun and Shadow series, Kingdoms of Tides and Twilight! Avaible now on Amazon!

If you enjoyed this book, please consider leaving a review on Amazon! Indie authors who don't have the marketing resources of large publishing houses depend on fellow readers to help spread their work so others can enjoy.

Interested in keeping up with Rachel Avery? Visit her website at www.RachelAveryAuthor.com!

Printed in Great Britain
by Amazon

42133620R00142